She made another awkward step and then another, but then her ankle wobbled. Her balance went and she was suddenly falling forward into Tom's arms.

He caught her, saving her from faceplanting on the floor, yes, but now she found herself in another strange predicament.

She was in his arms, head against his chest, hearing his heart pound inside his rib cage—and it was going fast. Probably from the shock of her falling, was all. She could feel the muscles in his body and smell his body spray, something masculine and earthy that performed wonders on her senses. When her cheeks flushed and she looked up into his eyes, something strange passed through them and she was so caught in his magnetism she forgot to pull away. Forgot to try and move. Forgot to try and operate her feet, because being in his arms like this? So close she could feel every breath? It was a heady place to be.

Dear Reader,

I really wanted to write a different specialty for this book and it occurred to me that I'd never written a firefighter. Initially, my hero was the firefighter and my heroine was the paramedic. But I knew that I wanted my heroine to have grown up as a tomboy due to having three older brothers—like me! And that was when I realized I needed to swap them over. Once I did that, the plot unfolded easily.

My mother used to despair that I wouldn't play with dolls or wear pretty dresses. I remember her tutting a lot! I was much more interested in building dens with my brothers, carving our own bows and arrows, and spending hours fishing in the river.

So, in this story, I had to add a despairing mother and a father that couldn't let go of his little girl. And then I developed my hero, Tom, who could see through Cara's armor and understand the hidden woman beneath the mask. Cara and Tom's connection was a pleasure to write and I hope you enjoy their story as much as I enjoyed creating it.

Louisa xxx

A DATE WITH HER BEST FRIEND

———

LOUISA HEATON

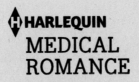

HARLEQUIN
MEDICAL
ROMANCE

HARLEQUIN®
MEDICAL ROMANCE™

Recycling programs
for this product may
not exist in your area.

ISBN-13: 978-1-335-73741-0

A Date with Her Best Friend

Harlequin Enterprises ULC
22 Adelaide St, West, 41st Floor
Toronto, Ontario M5H 4E3, Canada
www.Harlequin.com

Printed in U.S.A.

Louisa Heaton lives on Hayling Island, Hampshire, with her husband, four children and a small zoo. She has worked in various roles in the health industry—most recently four years as a Community First Responder, answering 999 calls. When not writing Louisa enjoys other creative pursuits, including reading, quilting and patchwork—usually instead of the things she *ought* to be doing!

Books by Louisa Heaton

Harlequin Medical Romance

Reunited at St Barnabas's Hospital

Twins for the Neurosurgeon

A Child to Heal Them
Saving the Single Dad Doc
Their Unexpected Babies
The Prince's Cinderella Doc
Pregnant by the Single Dad Doc
Healed by His Secret Baby
The Icelandic Doc's Baby Surprise
Risking Her Heart on the Trauma Doc
A Baby to Rescue Their Hearts
A GP Worth Staying For
Their Marriage Meant To Be
Their Marriage Worth Fighting For

Visit the Author Profile page at Harlequin.com.

To my three older brothers.
Thanks for sharing all the mud and drama!

CHAPTER ONE

CARA MADDOX WAS two sets in on a five-set high-intensity weights workout when her phone went off. The scary ringtone she'd allocated to her father filled the fire station's small gym and she debated whether to ignore the call. But familial duty got the better of her and she set the weights down with a sigh.

Wiping her face with a soft towel, she accepted the video call. 'Hi, Dad.'

Her father smiled at her. 'Hello, darling, how are you doing?'

He was sitting in a comfortable leather chair, and his background told her he was in the library of Higham Manor, her childhood home. Shelves and shelves of leather-bound books behind him reached from floor to ceiling.

He peered closer, then frowned. 'You look shattered. Are you taking care of yourself?'

'I'm in the middle of a workout, Dad.' She

checked her watch to note her heart rate and then paused her workout.

'Right. Of course. Got to stay fit in your type of job, I guess.'

'That's right.'

She stiffened slightly when he mentioned her job. Felt herself instantly go on the defensive. Her father had never been a fan of her joining the fire service. If he was calling just to have another go at her about it, or to suggest she change jobs, then she'd end the call. She really didn't have any time for that kind of nonsense any more.

'What can I do for you?' Best to get right to the point.

'I was wondering if you were going to come back home at the end of the month, for your mother's party? We haven't seen you in a long time, and it would be nice to see you.'

As he finished speaking, Michaels, her dad's butler, came into view, carrying a tray with coffee and biscuits.

'You're seeing me now.'

'Come now, Cara, you know it's not the same. It's your mother's birthday. She'd want you to be there.'

'She's been dead for years, Dad. She's not going to know whether I'm there or not.'

Her father bristled, waiting for Michaels

to leave the room before he began speaking again. 'But your family will. Our friends will. The *servant*s will. What will they think?'

'It doesn't matter what they think. I don't know them. They're your friends and associates. Not mine.'

'It's her *birthday*, Cara,' her father said, as if that should be enough explanation for everything. As if that should be enough motivation to get his daughter to do everything he wanted.

She felt guilty for trying to avoid it, but she'd been to many of those evenings before. They were meant to be about her mother, but all they were was a huge chance for her father to network with his friends and/or try to fix her up with the son of one of them. There would be a speech. Her mother would get a token mention. Heartfelt but short. Everyone would raise a glass and then her father's pals would go back to whatever business deals they were arranging, exchanging cards and contacts over cigars and brandies. And the entire time Cara would stand there, feeling awkward, trying to make conversation with a Tarquin or a Theodore—people she didn't know, who were all rather surprised that she did the job that she did.

It wasn't what they expected. She was the

daughter of an earl, and they expected her to be something other than a firefighter. The patron of a charity, perhaps? Someone who had a lot of lunches with her lady friends and cared way too much about handbags and nail polish. She was Lady Cara Maddox, after all.

But Cara didn't care for titles, or expectations, nor did she have lady friends. Most of her friends were guys. Her best friend was a guy. Tom Roker. Sweet, dear Tom. Handsome Tom. Paramedic. Father to a beautiful little boy called Gage. And widower of Victoria, who'd been willowy and tall and exquisite. Preened to perfection. The kind of woman Cara's father obviously wished his daughter would be more like. The kind of woman Cara could never be, which put Tom—dear, sweet, lovable, handsome Tom—completely out of her league.

Cara had always preferred the company of men. But that was what happened when you grew up with three older brothers and didn't quite fit in with the young ladies at your posh school. You hung around at rugby and polo matches, you laughed and joked with the boys, you competed with them, wrestled with them. You got to know your brother's friends and they were mostly guys. On the odd occasion when one of her brothers had brought home a friend who was a girl, Cara had had no idea how to talk to them! They'd seemed a different breed. Alien! Not interested in the slightest in Cara's topics of conversation, such as rugby or whether they wanted to arm wrestle! Clothes and designers and parties had been completely off her radar.

'I know. You don't have to remind me. I can remember all by myself.'

Her mother's birthday had also been her death day. For many weeks Serena Maddox had lain in bed, trying vainly to fight the ravages of breast cancer that had metastasised to her lungs, liver and bones. Cara had sat by her mother's bedside in those last few days when she was mostly asleep, listening to the fluid building up in her mother's lungs and throat, sponging her dry lips as her breathing got slower and slower, and she'd held her mother's hand as she'd taken her final, agonised breath.

It was a day etched into her brain. A memory filled with so much pain and so much guilt that she had never been the daughter Serena had dreamed of. Cara had let her mother down, and her father knew that, and she hated it when he used that to his own advantage.

'Come home, Cara. Your brothers will be

here. Clark is flying in from New York next week. Cameron will arrive a few days after that,' he said.

'And Curtis?'

'In Milan, still, but he promises he'll be back for the party.'

She could hear the tone in her father's voice. The tone that said, *I'm glad my boys have flown the nest and are upholding the Maddox name, but I do wish they lived closer to home.*

Her father, Fabian Maddox, Earl of Wentwich, was a proud man, and often boasted about his three sons, but Cara knew he would prefer to have them close by, so that the Maddox men could be a force to be reckoned with. Instead they were spread out across the globe, and their father could only preen, in their absence.

Clark ran a prestigious law firm in New York, specialising in family law and pandering to the rich, Cameron was in Cape Town, South Africa, running a business that built cruise ships, and Curtis was the CEO of Maddox Hotels, whose head office was in London. But she knew they were currently constructing a new hotel in Milan, which he was overseeing.

She spoke to her brothers often, and though

she'd never felt any judgment from them, she wondered if they, too, questioned her choice in jobs.

But being a firefighter was all she'd ever wanted to do. Ever since she'd been little, when a fire had broken out in the kitchens and her family and the staff had rushed from the building, only to watch in awe as fire-fighters rushed *towards* the flames. They'd arrived in huge fire engines, unloading equipment and hoses, and the flames licking out of the downstairs windows had soon been transformed into thick, grey smoke, billowing up into the sky.

She'd felt a nervous excitement at seeing them, had felt herself come alive watching them. It had been a heady feeling, and one she'd wanted to chase from an early age, even telling her parents, when she was just six years old, that she was going to be a fire-fighter. Oh, how they'd laughed at that, and Cara had felt flummoxed and confused by it. Why was it such a funny suggestion? Why did they all keep telling her that she'd change her mind when she got older?

She sighed. If all her brothers were coming back, if they were making the effort... She'd not planned on going this year. She'd done her duty, honouring her mother's birthday over the years. She'd been ready to start missing a few. Remembering her mother in her own way instead. Laying a wreath at her grave. Saying a few words, perhaps. Just... *remembering*, without having to stand around feeling uncomfortable, with people she didn't know, in order to fulfil some duty that her father had imposed.

Thankfully, she was literally saved by the bell.

The siren blasted out through the station. 'Gotta go, Dad.'

'But you've not given me your answer!' He leaned forward in his chair, filling the screen with his face.

'Sorry! Speak later!' And she ended the video call, pulling on a navy tee shirt and trousers over her workout clothes.

When that siren sounded you dropped everything.

Including any guilt.

In fact, she was grateful for it.

The siren meant that whatever was happening with her right there and then had to be put to one side for later. It wasn't important. What was important were the people who needed help. Those trapped in cars after an accident. Those who watched their businesses and often their livelihoods burning to the ground.

Green Watch often couldn't save someone's car or house or factory, but they could try to save lives—and that siren meant someone or something needed to be saved.

And that was what Cara lived for.

Tom Roker had just finished eating his sandwich when the call came through from Control about a house fire in Wandsworth and he was asked to attend.

'Roger, Control. ETA three minutes.'

'Roger that, four, three, two. Take care.'

He started the engine of his rapid response vehicle and reversed out of his spot, switching on the blues and twos as he raced towards the destination provided by his onboard computer.

The traffic was light today. The kind of traffic he wished he had to deal with most days. People got out of the way, they pulled over in the right place, the traffic lights were kind and he got to the destination quickly. His only problem was that cars lined both sides of the street. Pedestrians, neighbours—all had stopped or come out of their homes to gawp at the flaming spectacle of a house in full flame. Two fire engines blocked the street, and he could already see the fire crews doing their best to tame the fire. He wondered if Cara was on duty today?

It was a strange thing. He always hoped to see her, and yet also feared that she would be there. The idea of her running into a burning building... She might get a thrill out of it, but he didn't. Not until she was out again.

Tom sounded his horn to make people get out of the way, so he could get closer, and in the end managed to park behind one of the fire engines. Behind him, a normal ambulance arrived, and by the sound of the sirens he could hear many more emergency services were on their way.

He looked over at the house that was burning. It was a mid-terrace house, and the two front top windows were full of flame. It was licking at the bricks and there were holes in the grey slate roof through which more flame could be seen. Maybe the fire had started on the upper floor? On the ground floor the windows looked dark with smoke, occasionally strobed by torchlight as the fire crew made their way through the property, most probably looking for someone not accounted for.

His heart thudded at the thought.

People were crowding around the perimeter established by a police officer, filming it on their phones, their faces masks of awe and fear.

A firefighter wearing a white helmet came to meet him. He realised as he got closer that it was the Chief Fire Officer of Green Watch, known simply as Hodge, so Cara was most probably here somewhere, doing her thing.

'I've got Mum and Dad out, as well as two of the kids, but we're still looking for the third child. I think we're dealing with some basic smoke inhalation for most of them, though Dad's a COPD sufferer. He's also got a decent burn on his arm and left hand. They're over there in that appliance, receiving some oxygen.'

Tom nodded. Smoke inhalation could cause all manner of problems, from the simple to the most severe. Especially if the sufferer had medical issues to deal with, like asthma or COPD—chronic obstructive pulmonary disease. A patient with a respiratory issue could crash quickly, so it was important to keep a close eye on them.

'I'll do what I can.'

'Cheers, Tom.' Hodge headed back to co-ordinate efforts.

Tom made his way to the fire engine. Liam Penny, one of Cara's crew mates, was inside monitoring his patients. 'Hey, Liam. Whatcha got?'

'This is Daniel Webster and his wife Maria. The little one on her lap is Teddy and the brave girl over on your right is Amy.'

The mother removed her oxygen mask. 'Is there any word on Joey? Have they found him?'

Tom clambered in. 'They're still looking.'

'I need to be out there!' The mum tried to get up and push past him, but he managed to stop her.

'They'll come and find you if there's any news. Right now, I need you to stay here.' He replaced the oxygen mask. 'It's safer for you in here. The fire crews are doing their utmost to find him, but what I need you guys to do is try to stay calm and breathe in the oxygen for me.' He didn't need any of them running out there, getting in the way of the rescue operation. It was dangerous out there. 'I'll just put this SATs probe on your finger.'

The SATs probe measured oxygen and pulse rate. Normal oxygen levels for those without COPD were between ninety-four and ninety-eight percent. As he waited for the reading to appear, Tom used a tongue depressor and a pen light to look at the back of the dad's throat. The smoke inhalation and the COPD were more of a concern than the burn on his arm and hand and would need to take priority. He saw soot deposits. He'd need to be kept under observation in hospital for a while.

More than half of all fire deaths came from smoke inhalation. The smoke could cause inflammation of the airway and lungs, making them swell up and become blocked, and depending upon what types of gases were inhaled some of the inhalations would be toxic or poisonous. This dad was lucky he'd got out.

He began to cough, his eyes reddening and watering with the effort to try and clear his lungs, so Tom set him up with some extra oxygen and tried to coach him through his breathing. The two kids didn't look too bad. Shocked more than anything.

'Do we know yet how the fire started?' he asked Liam.

'We think it began upstairs, but the flash point… We're not sure.'

'I was burning candles,' the mum said, crying. 'And I… I think I might not have switched off my curling iron. Could that have started this? Is this my fault?' She looked at Tom in fear. Fear that he would tell her that it might be. But no one knew. Not yet.

Tom noted that her oxygen SATs weren't too bad at all. Ninety-three to ninety-four. On the lower end. 'We don't know for sure. Accidents happen all the time. You'll have to wait for the investigation results.' He moved the SATs probe from her finger to the dad's, whose laboured breathing sounded much more exhausted. He didn't like the man's colour.

At that moment a couple of paramedics arrived, dressed in their neon yellow jackets. 'Hey, Tom, what have we got?'

Relieved to have back-up, Tom handed over his patients, explaining about the dad's medical history and soot-covered throat. The paramedics offloaded the small family and escorted them to the ambulance, even though the mum kept protesting that she wasn't going to leave without knowing if Joey was okay.

Tom ached for her. But at that moment he saw a firefighter emerge from the building, carrying a dog.

'Bella! Oh, my God, Bella! How could we have forgotten about you?' The mum ran free of the paramedic and towards the Boxer dog, which was limp in the firefighter's arms.

Judging by the firefighter's walk, Tom knew it was Cara and, as always, he felt relief that she'd got through this fire okay. He knew it was her thing to run into the flames to help. It was her job, after all. But he always worried about her. She was a tough little cookie, who could hold her own, but that still didn't stop him from feeling he needed to protect her. Feelings of gratitude that she was out of the fire washed over him as usual. He wanted to see her face, but she still wore her rebreather mask.

Cara laid the dog down by the appliance and pulled off her own mask to get out some of the special equipment that he knew had been donated to them by an animal charity— a mask to fit around a dog or cat's face. He didn't realise he was holding his breath until he saw the dog trying to fight the mask and wagging its tail at its owner's approach.

'You might want to get her checked out by your vet,' Cara said as she gave the dog oxygen, pulling off her helmet and laying it on the side of the appliance.

Her hair was sweaty. Some of it was plastered to her skull, dark, as if it had been dipped in molasses, the rest was wispy and golden, almost auburn. Her hair, he often thought, was like flame itself. A mass of burning colours. Autumnal.

The first time he'd ever seen her with her hair loose and hanging down her back he'd realised he was staring, mesmerised by how beautiful it was. But that had been ages ago. In another time, it seemed. Back then…before he'd known her properly and they'd become the best friends they were now, he'd been attracted to her. How could he not have been? Cara Maddox was a stunning young woman. The sight of her had taken his breath away, but he'd been in no place back then to do anything about it. He'd been a married man. It would have been wrong.

So they'd just been associates. People who met at emergencies, until slowly they had become friends.

At that moment she met his gaze, noticing him, and her face broke into a hesitant, almost shy smile. 'Hey, Tom.' She touched her hair, as if ashamed of how it looked. As if she knew that it was sweaty and plastered to her head, that her pale skin had dark smears from the smoke upon it, that there were red marks on her face from the mask. That maybe she didn't look her best.

But to him she looked beautiful. The only problem was he couldn't tell her, in case she thought he was hitting on her.

'Hey. How was it in there?'

'Hot. Like it always is.' She laughed and unzipped her jacket a little.

'Any idea of what started it?'

'Not sure. But something upstairs in one of the bedrooms.'

One of the woman's neighbours had taken the dog, Bella, offering to look after it for the Webster family, so they could go to hospital in the ambulance and get checked out.

'How are all the patients?' Cara asked.

'Not bad. Smoke inhalation, minor burns. Dad will need an eye kept on him. He's got COPD, his SATs were low, and he has soot deposits on the back of his throat. Any sign of the missing boy?'

'House was empty apart from the dog, which I found whimpering under a bed.'

'Then where is he?' Tom frowned.

'Don't know. He could have gone out and not told anyone he was going, so they thought he was still inside.'

At that moment they became aware of a commotion amongst the crowd of onlookers. They both turned to look and noticed a young teenage boy struggling to get past the police presence.

'Mum? *Mum!*'

'Joey!'

'Mum!'

Mother and son ran into each other's arms, the mum bawling her eyes out with relief.

Tom and Cara both let out a breath, small smiles creeping onto their faces.

Cara turned to Tom. 'Happy ending in that respect.'

'Yeah… Ever feel like happy endings only happen to other people?' Tom mused.

Cara laughed. 'Oh, yeah.' She looked down at the ground, almost as if she couldn't think of what to say next. 'Are you okay?' she asked.

He shrugged. Everyone still expected him to be riddled by grief. 'Oh, you know how it is.'

She nodded. 'I do. How are things with Gage? All okay?'

'He's asking a lot of questions about his mum lately.'

'What do you tell him?'

Tom looked at the remains of the burnt house. The blackened bricks, the holey roof. Windows blown out from heat. The flames were gone and all that was left were plumes of thick, grey, swirling smoke, billowing up into the sky. Nobody had died today. Not here. And for that he was grateful.

'I tell him that she loved him very much. He doesn't understand if I tell him she got sick before she died, because he doesn't remember that. It happened so quickly sometimes even I struggle to understand it.'

'In those early days of Covid we all struggled to understand it. Don't be too hard on yourself.'

Cara laid a reassuring hand on his, before turning to look at what was happening with her crew. She had no idea what her touch meant to him.

'I'd better go. You going to be at The Crusader tonight?'

The Crusader was the preferred pub that all the fire crews attended—situated, as it was, just half a mile from their station.

'You bet. My parents have got Gage for a sleepover, so I'm free.'

She pulled her helmet back on, and gave him a warm smile and a wave before jogging back to her team. He watched her go, kicking himself for not saying anything to her.

Yet again.

The ambulance was pulling away, with the Webster family on board, and all Tom had to do was return to his rapid response vehicle and write his notes on the call.

The Websters had survived this terrible event and he was glad for them. It could have turned out so differently. A house and possessions could be replaced. People couldn't.

He thought about his son. How did you fully explain Covid to a near four-year-old? It would get easier, he hoped, as Gage got older and could understand more, but right now all his son knew was that he was the only child at his pre-school who didn't have a mummy. There were a few who didn't have dads, but mums…

Am I enough for my son?

Could he give Gage the cuddles and hugs he needed, the way his mother would have? He hoped so. Victoria had always shown her son affection. And he missed her, too. Missed her voice. Her presence. Which was strange, considering how they'd been with each other towards the end.

They should never have got married. They should never have got carried away with the romanticism of having been together since they were so young. The signs had been there, but they'd ignored them, because Gage had been on the way and Tom had wanted to do the right thing by Victoria and his unborn child.

Gage was his utmost priority now.

He couldn't be getting carried away with how he felt about Cara. He wasn't the best partner in the world for anyone to have, quite frankly. He'd failed Victoria and he couldn't go getting involved with anyone else right now. Gage wouldn't understand that.

And Cara? She would no doubt think badly of him if he declared his feelings for her so soon after losing his wife to Covid.

As the appliance pulled back into the station, the members of Green Watch descended from the vehicle and got into cleaning and maintenance mode. After every job they checked and maintained all equipment and cleaned the appliance if they'd attended a fire.

Cara began an audit of the equipment and checked the breathing apparatus supplies. She was glad of this respite. It was always a confusing moment after seeing Tom. Her feelings for him were confusing. He was her best friend, yes. Absolutely. She would give her life for him. But if she was being honest with herself then she had to admit that deeper undercurrents ran beneath the surface. Like a riptide of attraction that she had to fight every time they were together. But she was being respectful to his late wife. Acknowledging that he'd married his childhood girlfriend and had never looked at anyone else in his life so far.

Also—and she didn't like admitting this—

she knew that she could never be as good as Victoria.

She'd known Tom when he was married to his wife. Had socialised with both of them. She'd liked Victoria. Had seen why Tom was so in love with her. She'd been funny and warm. Friendly.

Cara had met Tom just half a year before Victoria had died. Their eyes meeting over the crumpled, steaming bonnets of two cars that had been involved in a head-on collision. At first she'd been startled by her reaction to a man she'd only seen for a couple of seconds. A man she had not yet heard speak. Whose name she didn't know. A man she had not spent any time with, nor yet seen smile.

She'd watched him clamber into the rear of one of the vehicles, to maintain a C-spine in an unconscious female driver who had suffered a head injury, and for a brief moment she had just stood still, watching him, mesmerised, her eyebrows raised in surprise at how she'd been frozen into place, stunned.

Is this lust at first sight? she'd mused, before her brain had kicked in and allowed the rest of the world to re-enter her consciousness. She'd heard instructions from the Green Watch Chief Fire Officer, Hodge, on how to tackle the incident. As she'd covered the driver with a blanket, to screen her from the glass of the windshield breaking as the Jaws of Life were applied, she'd stolen another glance at the paramedic who had intrigued her at first sight.

Dark hair. Dark lashes around crystalline blue eyes. High cheekbones. A solid jawline and a mouth that looked as if it was made for sin.

Cara had had to look away from him, pulse racing, face flushing, and she'd had to concentrate on what she was doing. Once the roof of the car had been cut off, she'd worked with Tom to co-ordinate the extrication of the driver. He had C-spine control, so he'd taken charge—counting them down, telling them when to get the backboard in. She'd helped to slide the patient on, then levelled the back board and helped carry her out of the car and onto a waiting ambulance trolley.

Then she'd turned away to help with the extrication of the second driver and her passenger, who were less injured, and conscious still, but who would no doubt have horrible whiplash injuries and dislocated shoulders to endure through the next few weeks. The engine block of their vehicle had crumpled inwards, trapping the legs of the driver, but thankfully had broken no bones. She'd been extremely lucky.

With the patients off to the hospital, and the crew organised to begin clearing up the equipment, she'd heard a voice behind her.

'Thanks.'

She'd turned. It had been him. Cara had done her best to keep her breathing normal, but it had been hard when he'd placed the full force of his gaze upon her. It had done alarming things to her insides. Her heart rate had accelerated. Her blood pressure had risen. Her mouth had dried to the consistency of a desert.

'Thanks to you, too.' She'd smiled. 'A job well done.'

She'd been pretty impressed that her tongue had still worked and that she'd not stuttered or tripped over her words. Because she had never felt this before. Not even with Leo.

He'd nodded. 'Absolutely. I'm Tom. I'm new.'

He'd held out his hand for her to shake and she'd taken it, glad that he couldn't ascertain that inside she felt molten.

'Cara. Nice to meet you. You've just moved to this area?'

'To be near my wife's family.'

My wife. Ah. Of course. A man like this wouldn't be single.

Disappointment had washed over her.

'Great. Well, welcome to the area.'

He'd thanked her and then headed back to his car, and she'd watched him go like a love-sick puppy. It had been then that Reed Gower, one of her Green Watch crew mates, had sidled up beside her, draped an arm around her shoulder and said, 'You know, if this were a cartoon your eyes would be on stalks and there'd be little love hearts on the end of them.'

She'd shrugged him off, annoyed that he'd noticed. 'Don't be ridiculous! He's new—I was just introducing myself, that's all.'

Reed had laughed as he'd walked away. 'Sure you were! Keep telling yourself that.'

After that she'd done her best to try and keep things distant, but he'd kept turning up at most of their shouts and eventually, as these things happened, someone on Green Watch had invited him to join them at the pub—The Crusader.

And Tom had turned up. With his wife, Victoria, in tow.

A small part of her had hoped that his wife

would be an ugly toad, but of course she wasn't. Victoria had been tall, long-limbed, gazelle-like, with wave upon wave of shiny honey-coloured, hair. And she'd had a very worthy job—but what else could Cara have hoped for? It had turned out that Victoria was a paediatric nurse. An *angel*.

Her perfect figure and shiny white teeth had been a hit with the guys, that was for sure, and very quickly Tom and his wife had become part of their group.

Until Covid had hit.

Emergency services had been classed as essential workers, so they'd still had to work, and somehow—terribly—Victoria had got Covid. The stunning Amazon Cara had considered her to be had been struck down, her fight against the disease complicated by asthma, and Victoria had been taken into hospital and placed on a ventilator.

Cara hadn't seen much of Tom after that. Understandably, he hadn't been at any of their shouts. She'd hoped he was at home, looking after his son, and not ill with Covid himself. There had been some talk of developing a vaccine, but the government had said it was at least a year away.

And then had come the news, passed down

from someone in the ambulance crew to Blue Watch, to Green Watch. Victoria had succumbed to Covid.

She was the first person Cara had personally known who had died from the disease and it had struck her harder than she'd ever imagined. It had come close, this invisible disease, and it could be fatal.

She had only been able to imagine how Tom had felt.

She hadn't wanted him to think that she didn't care enough about him to ring. So she'd rung Tom's house, left her condolences as an answerphone message. She'd hand-delivered a card through his letterbox, called his name, but there had been no answer and nothing else she could do.

When the funeral had been announced, she hadn't been able to go. Numbers had been extremely limited. But the funeral home had offered to stream the service online, so she'd watched it that way—attended that way whilst on duty at the station, watching on a laptop. Wishing she could be there to support her good friend Tom. She'd only seen him briefly in the stream, but he'd looked pale and shattered and her heart had ached for him and Gage.

He'd been off for about a month in total. The first job she'd seen him at, she'd gone to him and wished she could wrap her arms around him tightly, hug him and hold him in her arms for ever, but due to Covid restrictions the most they'd been able to do was bump elbows.

It hadn't seemed enough. Nowhere near enough. Her heart had still ached for him.

'How are you?' she'd asked him, standing a good two metres away.

'I'm okay. Thanks for asking.'

'You and Gage doing all right? Is there anything I can do?'

He'd shaken his head. 'No. Thanks. I got your card. It meant a lot.'

'I wanted you to know you were being thought about. I couldn't come to the funeral because of the restrictions.'

'I know.'

'I watched it online.'

'You did?'

She'd nodded, smiled warmly at him. 'If you ever need anything...even if it's just someone to talk to... I want you to feel you can call me. Any time and I'll listen. Rant. Rave. I'm here for you, okay?'

She'd seen his eyes redden and water, and had been touched that her offer had affected him so. If only she'd been able to reach out to hug him!

That all felt so long ago, but it wasn't. Not really.

So, yes, her feelings for Tom ran deep. There was attraction, but there was respect for all that had gone before—and the knowledge that no matter what she felt for him she could never live up to Victoria.

Cara was everything that Victoria had not been. Cara was a good head shorter than Tom's late wife. She had thick, strong muscles, from weightlifting at the gym every day, whereas Victoria had been lithe from Pilates. Cara had tattoos around both wrists and running up her forearms. Tom's wife had had none, and her only body modification had been pierced ears. Cara considered herself to be stocky, and there was nothing she loved more than to hang out in her gym clothes, or in boots and jeans and a tee. She'd never worn a heel in her life. Had never worn a pretty dress. Cara was a tomboy, through and through. Victoria…? She'd seemed to go everywhere in long, silhouette flattering dresses, that flowed and billowed around her, as if she was some sort of ethereal nymph. Graceful and elegant. Something Cara could never hope to be.

They were chalk and cheese.

So any feelings she had for Tom could never be reciprocated.

He just wouldn't see her the way she wanted him to.

CHAPTER TWO

RAIN POURED DOWN as Cara ran from her vehicle towards The Crusader, her jacket held over her head so that she didn't get wet hair. There was nothing worse than trying to enjoy a nice drink, but having cold, wet rain, dripping down the back of her neck.

She pushed open the heavy wooden doors, decorated with multi-coloured stained-glass, inhaling the familiar scent of hops and bar food. She shook her jacket as she scanned the bar area, searching for Tom.

Most of Green Watch were already there, and had command of both the pool tables and the darts board. She spotted Tom and a couple of other paramedics sitting at the games room bar, chatting. A few colleagues turned and greeted her, asking her to join them, and to add her name to the list at the pool table as she was such a good player.

'I'll just grab a drink first, then I'll be over.'

'We'll put your name up for you.'

'Thanks.' She smiled and headed over to the bar, deliberately going to where Tom was to say hi. Her heart fluttered in anticipation. He looked up as she came over and a broad, genuine smile broke across his face, lighting up those gorgeous blue eyes of his.

'Hey…look who it is. What can I get you?'

'Just a dry white wine, please.' She gave her order to the barmaid, Kelly.

'Still raining?' Tom asked.

She nodded. 'Cats and dogs.'

Kelly placed Cara's drink on the bar and Tom handed the barmaid a note.

'You playing pool tonight?'

'Always. You?'

Tom looked over at the chalkboard on the wall to check his name. 'Looks like I'm on just before you.'

'Ah, okay… Well, I'm planning to wipe the floor with you this evening. Make up for the last time.'

He laughed. 'You're going to have to bring your A game.'

'I know no other kind.'

They clinked glasses, then both took their drinks and walked over to the high tables and stools that surrounded the pool table area, taking a place by the window, which was steamed up on the inside.

'How's that family? Have you heard any more? The Websters?' she asked.

That was the thing with her job. You could be there for people, at the worst time of a family's life, but you didn't always get to hear the end of the story.

'The kids were sent home with an aunt, I think. Mum and Dad were kept in for observation, and I think the dad might be in there for a while.'

'What about his burn? Superficial? I never got a good look at it.'

'Second degree. The plastic surgeons were going to take a look, last I heard, because of how the burn was over his arm and hand. They don't want him to lose any movement or function.'

'Good. Well, I hope they're able to move on from this. It's going to be tough, losing their home, but the most important thing is that everyone survived. Houses can be replaced. People can't.'

'I think they may have some trouble moving on, though.'

'How so?' she asked.

She saw that some of the Green Watch crew were listening in to their conversation.

'They didn't have insurance.'

'What? Oh, no!' That was awful! Without insurance, they wouldn't have any money coming in to help get them somewhere else. Or to replace furniture. 'There must be something we can do for them?'

Cara's colleague Reed stepped away from the table and said, 'We could always do a fundraiser for them? Throw a party, or something? Ask for donations?'

Cara looked to Tom. 'Maybe… Do you think we could?'

He shrugged. 'I don't see why not. It would help them out, for sure.'

She thought about it. 'What sort of fundraiser, Reed?'

He took a shot, pocketing a striped ball, lining up his white cue ball perfectly for him to take on the black and win the game.

'Let me think…' He stooped low over the table, sank the black and won the game, commiserating with his opponent. 'We could ask for donations from local businesses? Auction them off?'

'We could auction promises,' Tom said. 'I saw this show once on TV where they did that. It was quite fun. Businesses donate a meal for two, for example, or a cleaner for the day, and people just auction something they're good at.'

Cara nodded. 'Like what? I guess I could run someone through a gym training session. What about you?' she asked both Tom and Reed.

Reed smiled. 'I could auction off a kiss.' He wiggled his eyebrows suggestively, causing everyone around them to laugh.

Hodge, their chief fire officer, who'd been listening over by the darts board, called over. 'Better offer an STD testing kit for afterwards, then!'

Reed pretended to be insulted, but he was smiling. 'Hey, that's…fair.' He laughed. 'I suppose we could always do one of those naked firemen calendars?'

Cara blushed at the idea.

Tom shook his head. 'They can't wait ages to get the money. They need it quickly. Whatever we arrange, it would have to be sooner, rather than later.'

Hodge nodded, thinking. 'I like the auction of promises idea. And getting companies to maybe donate items that the Websters need.'

Cara smiled. 'What do you think, Tom?'

'I'm happy to help in any way I can. I'm sure I can get a lot of the other paramedics to join in and spread the word if we have some sort of special night planned.'

'You could be a naked gardener, Tom!' Reed called, winking at Cara.

Cara felt her cheeks flush wildly at the suggestion. Tom? *Naked?* Now, that was usually an image she tried *not* to think about. Not because she didn't think he'd look good— because there was no way Tom wasn't beautiful all over—it was just because… Well, if she started thinking that way she'd never stop. And she was always trying to be respectful. Respectful of Victoria. Of Tom's loss. Of Gage. Thinking naughty thoughts could lead them down the wrong path, and there was no way in hell she was going to stupidly jeopardise her friendship with him by blurting out that she fancied the pants off him.

She hoped Tom hadn't noted the suggestive wink Reed had sent her way. She would have to have a word with him later and tell him to back off.

Cara sipped at her wine and just smiled at Tom, shaking her head as if to say, *What is he like, eh?*

'Tom. You're up next to play.'

Tom got up to the table and started racking up the balls for the next game. She watched him, wishing she could just look at him and see him as a friend, but these feelings for Tom were getting stronger every day. She had to find a way to control them!

Just as she was wondering whether she might have to avoid him for a bit—although did absence make the heart grow fonder?— the doors to the pub opened up, bringing in a burst of rain, and cold wind, and the sudden surprising outline of her father, hunkered down under an umbrella being held by his uniformed chauffeur!

At first Cara thought she was imagining things. Her father the Earl of Wentwich in a London pub? It couldn't be. Her eyes had to be deceiving her. She even gave them a rub—only to realise as she took another sip of her wine, that her father's doppelganger was headed straight for her.

'Cara, darling!'

Her cheeks flushed and she looked about her, keen for her crewmates not to realise who this was. She'd always tried to hide the fact that she was an earl's daughter, and although Hodge knew, he respected her enough to keep her secret, as she'd requested.

She'd worked damned hard to be accepted as someone who could give as much to being a firefighter as a man and prove to her crew that she could do exactly what they could.

Run into a burning building? *Check*. Carry a one-hundred-and-seventy-pound man in a fireperson's lift? *Check*. Keep up with the drills and the work and not expect any leeway for the fact that she was a girl? *Check*.

Cara dragged hold of her father's arm and quickly steered him in the other direction. 'What are you doing here?' she asked him in harsh whispered tones.

'I wanted to make sure you're all right.'

'Of course I am! How did you even know that I was here?'

'I tracked your phone using that app thing.'

Dammit! How had she forgotten to remove that after showing him how it worked?

'Dad, you shouldn't be here.'

'Why not? I thought it was time I met your team. Or are you ashamed of me?' He lifted his chin, smiling at her.

'Of course I'm not ashamed. But there are ways and means, Dad, and this isn't one of them.'

'No?' He stepped past her and headed straight for Hodge, reaching out his hand for a handshake. 'Hello. I'm Cara's dad.'

Hodge glanced at Cara. 'Lord Wentwich! Pleasure to meet you, My Lord. You have a fine daughter.'

Her father beamed. 'I like to think so, but

I wouldn't know because I hardly ever get to see her.' he said, directing his words in her direction, eyebrow raised.

Cara swallowed hard. All her work, all that time spent proving that she was just like everyone else, was about to crumble. She could sense it happening. It happened every time someone found out about who she really was. It changed people. It changed their behaviour towards her. And she didn't want her crew joking around, bowing and scraping every time she came into the room. It was stupid, and something she'd never liked.

When Leo had found out who she was, at first he'd been impressed. And then she'd quickly discovered that he was only staying with her for the fact that he could use her money and name to get the things that he wanted. He'd never been there for her. He'd never even been *attracted* to her. Something she'd realised in the most horrendous way. The things he had said…

'We were just talking about organising an evening to help a family that lost their entire home in a fire today,' Hodge told her father.

'*Really?* How awful. Our kitchens caught fire once. Terrible thing. I can't begin to imagine how they must feel.'

'We were thinking about a fundraiser. Getting businesses to donate furniture or goods, or raffle prizes. If you know of anyone who could help us out with that we'd very much appreciate it.'

Her father nodded, clearly thinking. Then his eyes lit up brightly as a thought occurred to him, and Cara knew instinctively that she was not going to enjoy the words that came out of his mouth next.

'The problem with those sorts of evenings is that you have to have the right kind of people attending. People with lots of disposable income, who are willing to throw crazy amounts around.'

'Dad—'

'You could hold it at my place—Higham Manor. In fact, we're holding an event at the end of the month to celebrate Cara's mother's birthday. We could make it a fundraising event and this family…the…er…'

'The Websters.'

He smiled his thanks to Hodge. 'The Websters could attend, too. In fact, let's invite them as my special guests.'

'That's amazing, Lord Wentwich! Thank you! That will certainly help keep our costs down.'

'Don't mention it. I'm pleased to help. Let's make it a masked ball. We could have music, dancing, and then the auction fund-raiser. You'll be there, Cara. Won't you?' He faced her with a smile.

Her father knew she wouldn't be able to re-fuse him now. He had her snared in a corner with no way out.

She would have to go. This wasn't just about her mother any more—it was about both her families. Her blood family and the people she thought of as her *real* family. Green Watch.

And Tom.

'Of course I will,' she said through grit-ted teeth as she stared at her father, both hat-ing him for pulling this trick to get what he wanted—her at Higham Manor—but also grateful to him for coming up with what had to be the best way for the Webster family to get funds for a new home.

Who was she to get in the way of a family rebuilding their lives?

Hodge, Reed, Tom and all the others beamed, but she could sense the questions from some of them, and could already see Reed and James Blake and David Garcia looking at her differ-ently.

They'd learned something new about her tonight. That her family had a manor house. That her father had a chauffeur.

That she was *different* from them.

Tom knew about her family already. It wasn't a secret to him. But he knew how much she didn't want the others to know. She hoped he would help protect her from their probing questions once her father had returned to his chauffeur-driven car.

'So it's settled, then!' Hodge beamed.

'Cara knows the time and date—don't you, darling?'

She nodded.

'I'll get my PR man on it first thing…start working on the donors in advance and seeing what prizes we can come up with.'

Hodge nodded. 'If you need us to help, just let us know.'

Her father clapped his hand to Hodge's shoulder. 'Don't worry. I can take care of everything. You guys continue to do your important work and concentrate on saving lives. I'll do the rest.' Her father shook Hodge's hand, then turned to her and kissed her on both cheeks. 'I'll leave you to your evening, then. It's been good to see you, Cara. I can't wait to see you at the ball. I know you won't let me or your mother down.'

And then he was gone, before she could say anything, and before she could blow her top. He did this every time. Took charge. He was used to it, of course, but it was one of the main reasons why she had left home as quickly as she'd been able to—to try and forge her independence. Why she'd tried to distance herself from her father's crazy influence.

They'd all left home. Cara and her three brothers. But of course her brothers were left alone to deal with their own lives. It was different for her. It was as if her father couldn't let go and kept interfering.

'Your Ladyship!' Reed bowed. 'I never knew I was in the presence of such class!'

'Give it a rest.'

She turned away and headed for the loo. She just needed a minute to gather herself. Splash her face with cold water and adjust to the fact that now everyone knew. It would no doubt get even worse once they'd actually been to Higham Manor and seen how she'd grown up. But what could she do?

As she stared at her reflection in the mirror she tried to tell herself that maybe it was better that it was all out in the open now. She waited to feel better about it, but nothing changed. She could still feel that tight, twisted feeling in her gut, and a rage against her father she knew she ought not to have. He was her one remaining parent, and she should be grateful for him, but his tight grip on her was like a chokehold sometimes.

Cara splashed her face with cold water, patted it down with paper towels and then girded herself for heading back outside. She yanked open the door and waiting outside for her was Tom. Dear Tom. Because he knew. Knew how she must be feeling.

Why wasn't she allowed to run straight into his arms?

'Hey. Want to get out of here?' he said, looking deep into her eyes. 'I have a getaway car waiting just outside.' He smiled.

He was so sweet. So perfect.

'Thanks. But, no. I need to face it. They were going to find out sometime, right?'

He nodded.

'Besides, I promised to thrash you at pool.'

She could think of nothing better than getting into Tom's car and driving away with him somewhere. Just the two of them. Pretending time didn't exist, their lives didn't exist, and it was just the two of them in each other's company for ever. They could park somewhere nice. Eat fish and chips together and stare up at the stars, holding hands or…

No. I shouldn't think of the 'or'.

He held out his hand and she looked at it as if he was offering her poison. *Take this and you'll be mine.* She wanted to take his hand so much! She often dreamed of it. The two of them walking in a park, as if they were a couple...

Only he wasn't offering his hand in that way, was he? This wasn't romantic. This was friendship. Support.

I'm with you. You've nothing to fear with me by your side. I'll protect you from their comments.

But she also knew that some of the crew—Reed, in particular—suspected she might have feelings for Tom, and if she returned to the pool table holding his hand she'd never hear the end of it.

'I'll be fine.'

She walked past him, towards her crew, head held high. Hoping that Tom understood.

Tom dropped his hand and watched her go. He had some idea of what she was feeling. Cara had always tried to forge her way through the world on her own merits, for which he was proud of her. He knew she hated it when her father railroaded her back into the world she'd used to exist in. A world in which she'd felt stifled and from which she had rebelled.

He followed her back to the pool table. It was set up, ready for him to break. Cara waited with her cue, determinedly chalking the tip.

Tom selected one from the rack on the wall and hefted it, feeling its weight, how it felt in his hands. Happy with his selection, he took the small cube of blue chalk that Cara had put down on the side, near one of the pockets, and chalked the end before bending down and lining up his white ball. He broke up the triangle of stripes and solid balls, sending them in all directions, pocketing a solid ball and giving himself another go.

'Are you rich?' Reed was asking Cara, downing the last of his pint.

Cara shook her head. 'No, I'm not. Look, I know you must all have questions, but there's a reason I've not spoken about that part of my life, okay? I'd prefer it if you all just left it alone.'

Tom had an easy shot he could take, but a part of him wanted to annoy Reed, so he went around the table to take a more difficult shot—which meant moving Reed from his position next to Cara.

'Excuse me.'

Reed backed off and headed over to the bar to refill his glass, and Tom smiled at Cara before taking his shot and missing.

Cara smiled back at him. 'Get ready to be thrashed,' she said.

He watched her pot ball after ball. She was very good. And he admired her for rolling with the punches and not leaving the pub after her father's visit. It would have been so easy for her to grab her jacket and run, but she hadn't. She'd faced it out. And he knew it was because she felt Green Watch were like her family. The family she'd always wanted. There was no way she was going to run from them.

Cara was down to her last ball before the black, but the striped ball rattled in the corner pocket and refused to go in. 'Damn!'

Tom laughed. His turn now. He looked at the layout of the balls on the table, planning his route of play. Each ball went in, one by one, with the white ball lining up for the next shot exactly as he'd intended, until he'd potted all his solids and was left on the black. It was at a tricky angle. If he missed it he would leave the table open for Cara to win the game.

'No pressure!' Cara said teasingly.

He glanced at her, warmth filling him at the smile on her face. The way her eyes gleamed in the light. He enjoyed his time with her immensely. Hours with Cara were never wasted.

She made him feel strong again. Something he'd lost since Victoria died. Losing her had left him feeling in limbo, struggling to be everything for his son Gage. And when Gage was finally asleep in bed there was hardly any energy left for him at all. He was exhausted.

Cara was helping to carry him through his grief. Always there for him. Speaking to him on the phone, or in a text, even in the later hours of the night when he was feeling particularly alone. He owed her a great deal that he could never repay.

That said, he wasn't going to throw this game. It would insult her, for a start.

Tom lined up the shot, steadied his breathing and struck the white ball. It connected with the black. Perfect angle. And the black headed over to the bottom right corner pocket and dropped in. Game won.

'Yes!' He turned in triumph to Cara, who laughed, and he pulled her into a hug, kissing the top of her head and trying not to be affected by the way her hair smelled of flowers, or how she felt in his arms. Fighting the urge to keep her in his arms longer than he should.

I need to let her go. Others are watching.

He stepped away from her, smiling, grabbing their glasses from the table. 'Another drink?'

She shook her head, looking strange. 'Just a lemonade or something, please.'

'Okay.' And he headed to the bar, determined not to look back at her, because his body was reacting in ways that it shouldn't do with a friend.

His mind interpreted the maelstrom of thoughts and feelings he was having.

He wanted more of Cara.

Only he couldn't.

And he would need to be strong to fight the feelings that were coursing hotly through his blood and toying with his concentration.

The call had come through as *'Person trapped'*. Which could mean anything. But the address was at a children's play park.

Green Watch clambered into their appliance and set off to their destination, lights flashing to get them through the burgeoning traffic.

Cara watched the houses and cars flash by, thinking over the events of the previous night. Her father showing up, playing the magnanimous hero and helping them out of a spot by offering to have a fundraising night at Higham Manor. Revelling in his role as a saviour. It was the sort of thing that he fed off, but the part he enjoyed most was interfering in her life. Why did he do it? And so often? Cameron, Curtis and Clarke didn't have the same problem.

As they pulled up at the park they jumped out to assess the situation, and quickly discovered that the person trapped was a teenage girl who had inserted herself into a baby swing as a dare. All her friends stood around her, drinking from cans and smoking, laughing at her predicament. Clearly, they all thought it was hilarious.

Hodge took point as always, forging his way through the girl's friends to assess the situation.

'What's your name, love?'

'Sienna.'

'And how did you end up in a baby swing?'

The baby swing was suspended by two thick metal chains, but the seat itself looked to be of moulded black rubber. Flexible, somewhat, but strong, all the same. Cara knew they wouldn't want to cut the chains or the seat, causing damage to the play park and therefore a headache for the local council, so this was probably going to be a pretty easy extraction by Green Watch using a bit of muscle power.

Once Sienna had explained the dare, Hodge asked her one final question. 'And are you hurt anywhere?'

'No.' Sienna's cheeks were inflamed and red as her friends recorded the situation, no doubt to put on social media later. 'Are you gonna cut me out with the Jaws of Life?'

Hodge shook his head. 'No need for that. We just need a couple of strong arms to get you out of this pickle.' He turned and motioned to Cara and the others. 'Cara? You and Reed can lift and I'll hold the seat in place.'

'Okay.'

There was a lot of squealing from Sienna. Laughter. Complaining that they were tickling her or pinching her as they hauled her upwards so Hodge could pull downwards on the rubber seat. The chains clanked and clanged as they swung this way, then that, until eventually they freed the embarrassed teen and set her back on her feet.

'There you go,' said Hodge. 'And next time you want to play on the swings stick to the ones meant for older kids, yes?'

Sienna nodded. 'Thanks.'

They headed back to the appliance. If only all their jobs could be so easy. If only all their calls could be as simple as getting people out of sticky situations.

Perhaps Cara needed a fire crew to help her out of the situation with her dad?

Back at the station, Cara had barely got the kettle on when her mobile phone, which she'd set on silent, vibrated in her back pocket. She pulled it out and saw her dad's name. She let out a breath, not sure that she wanted to read the message. What could it be now?

Hey, Cara. Just a reminder about the fundraiser. It may be for the Webster family, but it's still your mum's evening, too, and she would have loved to see you attend dressed as a lady. It's what she would have wanted. A dress and heels, please. Have your hair done. Make-up. I'll pay. Just do her proud.

Cara stared at the phone in disbelief. He'd had to go there! Getting right to the one thing that he knew Cara felt guilty about!

Serena Maddox had *dreamed* of having a daughter after three boys. She'd loved her sons—of course she had—but she'd longed to have a daughter she could dress in pink and play dolls with, have a special bond with. And Cara disappointed her from the get-go.

She'd very much been a tomboy—playing in the mud with her brothers, going hunting, making dens, playing rough, happy in jeans, not interested in anything remotely pink, and certainly not in dolls or dresses or shoes or handbags.

She'd refused to be railroaded in such a way. It had always been a disappointment to her mother. And when her mother had died Cara had felt the guilt of never giving her what she'd wanted. Not even for one day. And that guilt had caused her to stay in her own lane even more. Because what was the point in doing anything different now? Her mum wouldn't get to see it.

She'd started going to the gym even more, working out, lifting weights. Punishing herself. She'd got tattoos. Hey, she'd already failed at pleasing her mother—why not go for it?

But it had all been grief. Just her way of coping. She wasn't that bad now—though she was still a stranger to anything other than boots or trainers. And pink? There was nothing in her life that was pink. Cara liked black and grey. Didn't own a single handbag. She would feel like a complete alien from another planet if she had to go dress-shopping. Or shoe-shopping! She'd much rather hang out at the gym. The only shops she frequented were grocery stores and bookshops.

At that moment in time, she hated her father.

So she punched in the number of the only person she knew she could talk to about this.

Tom.

He answered on the first ring. 'Hey. How are you doing?'

It was so good to hear his voice. She'd not seen him since the night at the pub and she'd missed him. Just hearing his warm voice now made her want to hug the phone tight to her ear and cry.

'Not great,' she said.

'Oh. What's up? Anything I can help with?'

'I hope so. Can I pop round later? I'd like to see you.'

There was a pause as she heard him talk to someone. Gage's voice in the background. 'Sure. I'm just getting Gage ready for bed. When is your shift over?'

'In half an hour. Can I come straight round?'

'Course you can. But Gage might be sleeping, so text me when you're here, so the doorbell doesn't wake him up.'

'Thanks, Tom.'

She ended the call, feeling a little better.

Tom always made her feel good. Always listened when she had a problem. And she thought that he got a lot out of their friendship, too. She was company for him, she thought. Female company...which he had to miss after losing Victoria, right? Someone to talk to in the evenings after Gage had gone to bed.

When she got to his house he let her in, and she went straight into his arms for a long hug. It was as if he knew she needed comfort, and for a while she just stood there, head pressed against his chest, listening to the regular, methodical beat of his heart, her eyes closed in bliss, just breathing him in. He felt so strong. So sturdy. A steady presence.

She wasn't sure how long they stood there in silence, but eventually Tom asked her if she wanted to go into the lounge and he'd make her a drink.

If she was honest, she could have stood there in his arms all night. Not talking. Not speaking to each other. Just communicating through the hug. The need to be held. To be comforted. To feel safe and loved and not judged. For there to be no demands made by either person.

'Sure. Okay.' Reluctantly, she let go of him

and followed him into the lounge, where she sat down on one of his comfy sofas.

'Tea? Coffee? Something stronger?' he asked with a smile from the kitchen doorway.

'Tea's fine, thanks.' She let out a sigh.

'Is it your dad?' he asked when the kettle was on and he'd come back to the lounge whilst waiting for it to boil.

She smiled wryly. 'Who else?'

'What's he said now?'

Cara pulled her phone from her pocket and showed Tom the text.

'Emotional blackmail. Nice.' He handed the phone back. 'What did you say to him?'

'I've not answered yet. I know he's not asking for a big thing. Wear a dress. Wear some heels. Look like a proper fricking lady for a change! But it's just the way he brought my mother into it, you know? He knows how I felt when we lost her and he's using that guilt against me.'

Tom was silent for a moment, as if searching for the right words. 'I wouldn't be happy if someone used me like that either. I'd probably not speak to that person for a while. But this is different. It's your dad. He's the only parent you've got left.'

'Yeah…'

'If you want to turn up at that evening

wearing camo paint and army fatigues, I'll back you one hundred percent...' He smiled.

Cara laughed.

'But if you do decide to give him what he wants, to get him off your back, then I'll back that decision also.'

She sighed. 'What do you think I should do?'

'It's not my decision to make. But if you do go the dress route, I'd take the opportunity to tell your father he can never use your mother against you ever again.'

'Agreed. But how would I even know how to wear heels? I'd probably break my ankle.'

'Hey, come on. It's one night. A couple of hours at the most. You run into burning buildings, Cara! The bravery that takes? I couldn't do it. But I have no doubt that you can do this.'

She looked into his eyes. Saw the warmth there. The love. The support. If he had belief in her, then maybe she should have belief in herself too.

'Okay.'

'You're going to do it?'

'I'm going to do it!'

She laughed with relief. Glad that Tom had helped her see sense. He was right. It was one night. Three hours? Four? And then it would all be over and she could tell her father that she'd done her bit and he needed to let her live her life as she pleased in future.

'Let's have biscuits with that tea,' said Tom. 'I think I have some chocolate digestives to celebrate.'

'Rock and roll.'

CHAPTER THREE

TOM HAD JUST got back into his rapid response vehicle, after treating a suspected cardiac arrest, when a call came through that there had been a multi-car pile-up on one of the main roads in Battersea. He flipped the switch for his blues and twos and told Control to show him as attending, ETA five minutes.

'Roger that. Police and fire crew are also en route.'

The streets were thick with traffic, and in some parts he had to wait as vehicles already in the jam tried to find a way to move aside, to let him through. Moments like this taught him patience. There was nothing he could do, and it was too late now to go back and try an alternative route. In front of him, drivers tooted their horns at one another, and a few wound down windows to make hand gestures to other drivers, telling them to move over a bit more. And slowly, slowly, the cars parted and created a very narrow lane for him to drive down.

He inched his way along until he was finally able to get through the lights, hit a right and drive down a road that was thankfully much clearer and traffic was flowing. This was better. But his anxiety was high. The traffic jam had caused him a significant delay and time counted. Someone could be trapped inside a vehicle, losing blood, losing precious seconds in which their lives might be saved.

But despite this he knew he had to use caution still. Every junction, every crossing, every school that he passed could be a potential site of danger for pedestrians or cyclists or other motor vehicles that simply didn't see or hear him. Despite the lights and sirens, it was amazing how many people could be in their own little world when they were out and about. It wasn't unheard of for emergency vehicles to end up in a pile-up themselves.

But he was getting closer.

Then the traffic was beginning to snarl up again, and he had to inch through, until he managed to park behind a police car that itself was parked behind a fire engine.

The street was lit with strobing red and blue lights as he grabbed his jump bag, slipped on a high vis vest and walked towards the accident.

He sucked in a breath at the sight of it.

A blue car lay on its roof, facing in the wrong direction, steam hissing out of its engine. A silver car was on the other side of it, its front crumpled in, airbags deployed. A white van was parked askew to the left of them, the driver's door hanging open, and behind them a lorry that had obviously skidded to avoid them had crossed over into the wrong lane, hitting a small red car.

He could see Hodge, striding around in his white helmet, which told him that Cara had to be on the scene somewhere. Maybe one of the team currently gathered around the blue car. All around police were trying to establish a perimeter, as nosy onlookers gathered. Some officers were comforting people kerbside. Were they drivers? Walking wounded?

Tom got Hodge's attention and the chief fire officer came over to him.

'Hey, where do you want me?'

Hodge pointed. 'The driver of the blue car needs the most attention. She's trapped inside the vehicle, unconscious, breathing sounds bad, respirations are really low. We've got her on oxygen and Cara's holding C-spine. There was a child in the back, strapped into a baby seat. We've got her out. Seems fine, just a little shaken up, but she will need a check. Driver of the white van is fine—he avoided impact, as did the lorry driver. The guy driving the silver car has whiplash, and the passengers of the red car are in shock and have a few cuts and bruises.'

'Most of them have been lucky, then?'

'If you call a car crash lucky, yeah.'

Tom hurried forward towards the blue car that was upside down on its roof. He acknowledged Cara with a quick smile. 'Morning.'

'Good morning,' she said.

'We really need to stop meeting like this.'

She smiled at him as she lay on the road on her side, her arms within the car, holding the driver's neck. 'We must.'

'Was she unconscious when you got here?' asked Tom.

'Yes.'

'And hasn't woken up?'

'No. And her breathing has been slow and erratic. I can hear a wheeze.'

Thankfully, Cara and her crew had already got the driver on oxygen. Tom reached through the broken glass and past the deflated airbag to place his stethoscope on the patient's chest.

'Agreed. I think she's asthmatic.'

He felt dread wash over him. Something he always felt now, when he had to attend to an asthmatic, since the death of his wife.

Asthma was the complication in Victoria's medical history that had led to her death from Covid at the beginning of the pandemic. Hearing this woman wheeze, seeing her pale face, reminded him of his wife's attacks.

There'd been one time when she'd totally collapsed. It had been Christmas, and they'd invited both sets of parents over to their house. Victoria had woken that morning feeling breathless. They'd argued, because Tom had said they should cancel their guests, as clearly she wasn't well, but Victoria, not willing to let people down on Christmas Day, had simply shaken her head, used her inhalers and said she'd power through. He'd helped her peel veggies and prepare the table, and then he'd set off in the car to fetch his parents, who didn't have a vehicle, leaving Victoria at home.

She'd promised, she'd stay sitting down, reading a book or watching TV, until he got back. Only when he had returned they'd walked in, full of Christmas cheer, with his parents calling out 'Merry Christmas!', only to find Victoria lying on the floor of the kitchen, face pale, wheezing terribly, close to losing consciousness.

He'd called an ambulance so fast! His parents had taken over the cooking and when Victoria had got better and was finally allowed home, they all had Christmas dinner really late that night.

Had *this* woman been suffering, but thought she was okay to drive her car? Or had the attack started in the car? Maybe even caused the crash?

Tom didn't know, but the woman's airway was his primary concern. ABC. Airway. Breathing. Circulation. Airway came first. He organised a nebuliser first.

'Let's get a cervical collar on.'

He pulled the one he had from his bag and positioned it around the woman's neck. Then he could continue with his primary survey.

Cara, now free from holding the C-spine, joined her crew to help with prepping the vehicle for extraction.

Tom could see cuts on the woman's face and arms, but had no idea if she'd sustained any broken bones, and he wouldn't know for sure until they got her free of the vehicle. He attached a SATs monitor to her, checking her oxygen levels, and then Cara was asking him to move back, so they could safely break the glass around the vehicle, ready for cutting.

He stood back, knowing he could do no more until she was free, but he was worried. Focused. He wanted her out of the vehicle so he could treat her properly, but this next bit would take some time.

Cara's crew had already stabilised the vehicle, so that it wouldn't move as they cut through the metal. They were cutting through the struts to take the stress off the roof of the car, freeing it to make it easier to free the patient.

Cara used power tools to cut through the fender and expose the door hinges, before Reed removed the doors all round. Then they cut the post above the door hinges and began using another power tool to lift the car free from the dashboard and create even more room, whilst Hodge continued to stabilise the vehicle from the rear.

All Tom could hear was the crunch of metal. He checked his watch. This was time-critical. The woman could stop breathing at any moment. Behind him, other ambulances had arrived and were checking the walking wounded, so he could retain his focus on the asthmatic patient.

He wondered what her name was. Where

she was going. What she'd thought her day would involve when she'd set off this morning. Had it just been another day? Who did she have worrying about her?

Cara's crew had secured the vehicle once more, then moved the car seat out of the way, and were now calling for the backboard so they could slide it in through the rear of the vehicle to get the patient out without causing more damage to the spine or neck.

'Easy now!' Tom called as he helped them guide her out.

Thankfully her legs weren't trapped, and they looked in reasonable shape, though there were cuts to her knees. He had to hope there weren't any internal injuries, but he wouldn't find out until later.

Once she was free and on a trolley, he rechecked his primary survey. Her oxygen levels were low and she was at risk of going into serious respiratory arrest.

'Get her to the hospital now!' he instructed the paramedics helping him.

He had to stand back and watch them take her. He'd done all he could, though he felt, as he often did when seeing an asthmatic patient, that he hadn't done enough. He'd given her medication in the oxygen, but that seemed pathetically little help. It always did—especially if the patient was too far gone into their attack and didn't respond to it.

Would she survive? He didn't even know her name. He hated feeling this way.

He felt a hand on his arm. 'Tom? Are you all right?'

Cara. Her soft voice was balm for his soul. He nodded. Smiled.

'Are you sure? I know this must hit home for you. I'm sure she'll be okay.'

'Thanks. I hope so.'

'Hey, do you want me to pop round later? I could bring a takeaway. Your choice.'

'I don't think I'm in the mood for takeout.'

'How about I come round early and take Gage off your hands for a bit? We haven't played footie together for ages.'

'He'd love that. He loves it when you come. Maybe we should all go out? The fresh air will do me good.'

She smiled. 'Okay. I gotta go now, so I'll see you later? About five-thirty?'

'Perfect.'

He watched her return to her team. They had work to clear up. Their job wasn't over just because the patients were all out.

He was thankful for Cara. Thankful for her friendship. Her insights into his emotional wellbeing. She'd realised how treating an asthmatic would affect him. How the sound of an asthmatic wheeze often chilled his blood, because it reminded him of Victoria's battles with the condition.

He headed back to his car, exchanged his empty oxygen tank for a full one from an ambulance that had not yet left the scene, and then sank into his vehicle to write up his notes.

But as he sat in the car he tried to remember the last time he'd spoken to Victoria. What had their last words to each other been? He couldn't remember. *Why* couldn't he remember? Was his brain trying to protect him from something? Or was it something mundane? He felt their last words ought to have been important. *I love you. I'll miss you. Get well soon.* Only he had a sneaking suspicion it hadn't been those. He'd been panicking over her worsening breathing. Insisting she call a doctor. But she'd refused, saying it wasn't that bad, and had isolated herself in their bedroom whilst suggesting he slept on the couch—so he didn't get sick, so he could take care of Gage.

By the time he'd got an ambulance and the crew had assessed her, she'd barely been able to talk. Her eyes had been wide with fear from the strain of breathing and trying to get desperately needed oxygen into her lungs. The paramedics had talked to her as they'd carried her down the stairs in a portable chair. Reassuring her. Telling her she was doing fine. Not much further to go. Then Gage had begun to cry, frightened by these strange men in his home, no doubt sensing the tension and upset, and Tom had been trying to soothe their son. Holding him tight, stroking his hair, telling him to say goodbye to Mummy.

Had he said anything important to Victoria? Or had he missed the opportunity, believing that he would be able to speak to her later, on the phone? An occasion that had never materialised, because when they'd got her to the hospital they'd anaesthetised her and put her on a ventilator and she'd never come off it.

So their last words to each other must have been before that. They could have been anything!

'I'd better sleep downstairs, then, so I can look after Gage.'

'Do you need anything? A cup of tea?'

'I'll leave your plate just outside the door. Try and eat.'

Maybe those words said *I love you*, only in a different manner?

He hoped so. He hoped she'd interpreted

them in that way. Because he knew that when he *had* told her that he loved her she hadn't been able to hear him. Because she'd been unconscious, with a tube down her throat, and dying. He'd had to say it over the phone, with a nurse holding the handset to her ear. But by then it had been too late.

He hoped the lady today had someone who would sit by her bedside. Someone who loved her. That they would get the chance to say to each other all the things they wanted to say.

Because it was awful when you couldn't tell someone how you really felt.

Cara rang the doorbell, smiling in anticipation of hearing Gage race his father to the door, so that he could greet their guest first.

She saw his little figure through the glass and felt her heart swell. Gage was a wonderful little boy, delightfully happy and curious and funny, despite all that he had gone through.

He stretched to reach the door handle and finally swung the door open. 'Cara!' He leapt up at her and she caught him in her arms, swinging him up high, easily, and whirling him around.

'Hello, you! Are you ticklish today? Let me see!' And she put him down on the ground and began to tickle him under his arms, causing him to giggle and laugh and collapse on the doormat hysterically. 'Hmm… Maybe… What about here? Or here?'

Gage laughed and laughed, squirming, enjoying the game, and then suddenly Tom was there, looking great in dark jeans and a white tee, and she felt the usual wave of heat and awareness wash over her, taking her breath away.

She released Gage and stood up straight. 'Hey.'

'Hey.' He smiled back, and she was glad to see he seemed a little brighter than earlier at the accident.

'Want to come out and play?' she joked.

'Let me just grab our jackets.'

'And a ball?'

'Ah, yes. Of course. Gage? Go and fetch your football from the box by the back door, please.'

'Yes, Daddy.'

Tom ruffled his son's hair as he ran past.

'He's getting big,' said Cara. 'What are you feeding him?'

'He'll eat anything. The boy's not picky. Must be a growth spurt.'

Gage came back, ball tucked under his arm. 'Are we going to the park?'

'We certainly are,' she answered. 'Come on, you. I need you to show me your moves and what you've learned since I saw you last.'

As they walked down the street to the park, Gage in the middle, holding Cara's hand on the left and Tom's hand on the right, Gage talked non-stop. About keepy-uppies, how many goals he'd scored against his dad at the weekend, how he was going to be a pro footballer when he was older.

Cara looked over his head at Tom to smile and share in the wonder of this little boy. She loved little Gage. He was perfect. Just the kind of kid she'd wish to have herself, if she was ever lucky enough to have a family of her own. Not that that was looking likely. Men didn't seem to notice her, which only reinforced her doubts about her own attractiveness.

Besides, she was always at work, her body and face hidden behind her firefighter's uniform and helmet. The only men who did notice her were her crew, and none of them were single. They were all married or in long-term relationships, apart from Reed, and they only saw her as a friend and colleague. Someone they could trust with their lives. Who had their backs. They didn't see her as potential love interest. Did they even think she was pretty?

They were protective of her, though. Like extra big brothers. Which was kind of nice, but could be scary for guys who did take an interest. Like Leo, for example. Her crew mates hadn't been fond of him. *Suspicious* might be a better word for how they'd felt about Cara's ex. And when Leo had ripped out her heart and walked away without so much as a backward glance, they'd been queueing up to go visit him and *'have a word'*.

She'd appreciated the offer, and the sentiment…but by then she'd felt so humiliated, she'd wanted nothing further to do with him.

Cara stole glances at Tom as they chatted with Gage and wished that he saw her as more than a friend. There'd been moments where her hopes had been raised. Once, she'd caught him looking at her oddly as she'd helped him put together a treehouse in the back garden. The way he'd been looking at her had made her feel self-conscious.

'What?' she'd asked.

'Oh…nothing. I was just daydreaming.'

'About what?'

He'd shaken his head. *'Nothing.'*

She'd returned to hammering in nails, hold-ing two of them in her mouth, but it had been enough to make her feel that she'd been assessed and found wanting.

Would Victoria have helped him build a treehouse? No. She'd have left him to it. Brought out the occasional cup of tea and told him how good it was looking, but that would have been all. And yet there she'd been, in the scruffy tee shirt she used when she was decorating and some cargo pants, covered in sawdust and sweat!

Hardly attractive!

Tom was so handsome and so deserving of some happiness and she felt she could provide it. But she didn't have many friends outside of the fire service, and she didn't want to ruin the friendship she had with Tom by complicating it. Besides, he probably wasn't ready to date yet. He was too busy being a father to Gage and he would *never* be interested in her. No matter how much she wished he would.

The park wasn't that busy, and they managed to find a space where they could kick around the ball. Gage and Tom used their discarded jackets as goal posts and Tom went into goal, leaving Cara and Gage as opposing team members, desperate to score. Around them, birds sang in the trees and squirrels searched the ground for acorns or whatever it was that squirrels searched for. Gage sent one shot wide, the ball flying over to a bunch of oaks, and a grey squirrel shot halfway up a tree trunk and peered at them as if in reproach.

'I'll get it!' Gage said, running after it, his little legs pumping hard. He picked up the ball and came back, throwing it past her to take a shot at goal.

'Hey!' Cara laughed and let him take his shot.

Tom paused and let the ball roll past him and score, pretending he'd been too slow to stop it.

'Yay! One nil to me!' Gage lifted his tee shirt above his head, like footballers did on television, and ran around until he fell over, collapsing with laughter.

Cara scooped him up, righted his tee and then tried to dribble the ball past him. Gage tackled her. She let him have it and he scored again.

'Oh, you're too good for me!' she said, hands thrown in the air, and then she, too, collapsed onto the grass.

Gage jumped on her and she scooped him up above her, whirling him around like an airplane. Eventually Tom took him from her arms and whirled him to his feet.

'I'm exhausted. Who fancies ice cream?'

'Me, me, me!' Gage said.

Tom raised an eyebrow at Cara. 'Fancy a mint choc chip?'

'You know the way to my heart!' she joked, wishing that he really would find the way.

Maybe he would one day. Maybe she was wrong to think he would never see her in that way. One thing she knew for sure was that Tom was worth waiting for…and if it was meant to take some time, then she was okay with that. Being his friend for now would have to be enough. She just hoped he wouldn't do something stupid, like fall in love with someone else, so she'd have to stand there on the sidelines and watch him with another woman.

Tom held out his hand, which she took, and he hauled her to his feet.

They gathered the jackets and headed towards the ice cream van at the other end of the park. One mint choc chip, one strawberry and one chocolate ice cream later, they were sitting on the benches by the public aviary cages, watching the budgies flit from perch to perch as they licked their ice creams.

'So, have you decided what you're going to wear yet for the ball?' Tom asked.

She sighed. 'No. I keep trying to ignore it.'

'You've only got to the end of the month.'

She changed the subject. 'What are *you* going to wear?'

'I have a tux tucked away somewhere. All I have to do is find a mask.'

She stared at him for a moment as an idea formed. Was she brave enough to ask? Would this be expecting their friendship to go to places it wasn't ready to go?

'Would you help me?'

'With what?'

She blushed. She didn't normally ask for help, and for some reason this seemed like a really big thing to ask of him. It seemed… intimate.

'Help me find a dress? I have no idea what type of thing to look for and I'm just not used to going into those types of places.'

He laughed nervously. 'You mean shops?'

'Girly places.'

'You think *I am*?'

'Well, you must have sat around waiting for Victoria to shop sometimes? Offered an opinion on an outfit? I would like a male opinion.'

She honestly thought he was going to say no. He seemed to think about it for an inordinate amount of time. Looked as if he was going to turn her down. As if he was trying to think of an excuse without hurting her feelings. Maybe she should just let him off the hook? Tell him she was being silly? Of course he didn't have to go shopping with her! What kind of man enjoyed going clothes-shopping with a girlfriend? None that she knew.

'Okay.'

'You will?' She brightened. At the fact that he'd said yes and the fact that it meant spending a lot more time with Tom.

'Sure. Why not?'

Cara flung her arms around him and kissed him on the cheek. 'Thanks!'

She released him to lick her ice cream, her body thrumming with excitement. One question down. Now to ask the next.

Gage got up and idly dawdled over to the bird cages for a closer look.

Cara lowered her voice. 'Could I ask you one more thing?'

'Sure. Go for it.'

She hoped she wouldn't blush. She failed. Miserably. 'Would you come as my date?' Her cheeks bloomed with heat and she almost couldn't make eye contact with him. 'Only my dad will try to pair me off with someone if I turn up alone. Last time it was with this dimwit called Hugo. The son of one of his best friends. All he could talk about all night was stocks and shares. I was bored rigid and totally embarrassed. With you there… I could avoid that.'

'You mean you don't want to hear my scintillating take on the stock market?' he teased.

He could read her the phone book and she wouldn't mind.

'No, thanks.'

They both laughed, tension released, but she crunched into her waffle cone, painfully aware that he hadn't said yes yet.

'So…you want me to pretend to be your boyfriend?'

She checked to make sure Gage couldn't hear what they were saying, but he appeared to be enamoured of the brightly coloured birds flitting from perch to perch. 'Yes. I know it's asking a lot, and if it makes you uncomfortable then please feel free to say no. I'd totally understand. I'd—'

'I'd be honoured.'

Cara stared at him, fighting the impulse to drop her ice cream cone and plant her lips directly on Tom's. Her heart pounded in her chest.

'Thanks.' she said, instead. 'That means a lot to me.'

Tom shrugged. 'It's no big deal. It's just pretend, right?'

She nodded. 'Right.'

* * *

'It's just pretend, right?'

That sentence kept repeating over and over in Tom's mind all night. Condemning him and teasing him in one stroke.

Cara was amazing. Beautiful, clever—and she loved Gage almost as much as he did! But…what would people say? It hadn't been two years since he'd lost Victoria, and everyone had assumed everything was great between them. Childhood sweethearts? What could possibly go wrong?

People had fallen in love with that idea. They'd thought it was sweet and romantic and perfect. How would they react if they knew what had truly been going on?

He'd believed at the time that marrying Victoria when she discovered she was pregnant was the right thing to do. And it had been! It had allowed him to watch Gage grow up in the same house as him every day. To experience his milestones first-hand. He'd been there for his first word—*Dada*. His first faltering steps. But he'd also seen Victoria change. Almost as if she'd resented having become a mother so soon.

She would palm Gage off on him the second he walked through the door, so she could go off and have 'girl time' with her friends.

They'd argue over simple things Her appearance had mattered to her more than anything else sometimes. She'd spent crazy amounts of money on hair extensions and dresses and heels she never wore, when he'd given her that money for the things Gage needed.

He'd tried so hard to be the best partner he could, but it had never seemed to be enough. She'd always found him wanting, no matter what he did to try and make her happy, and so he'd given up trying. Working long hours. Taking extra shifts. He'd told himself he was doing it for his boy, so they could afford everything he wanted in life, but really he'd been doing it because it was easier to be at work.

What would people think if he started to show that he had feelings for someone else so soon? He didn't want to dishonour Victoria's memory. And Cara? She'd think badly of him for fancying her, surely.

Maybe he was reading more into his feelings for her than he should? Maybe he just *thought* he had feelings for her because she was such a good friend? Because she was so supportive and kind and enjoyed spending time with him and Gage?

I'm just misreading the situation. Grateful for her kindness, that's all.

That was why he hadn't turned down her offer to go dress-shopping with her. He'd thought about it! Going dress-shopping with Victoria had been downright exhausting! Sitting in chairs, watching her go in and out of changing rooms, hearing her asking him if he preferred the scarlet or the crimson…

'They're both red, Vic. Just pick one!'

He had been going to say no. Initially. Watching the woman he had strong feelings for putting on pretty dresses? What if he slipped up and said something incriminating?

And then he'd thought about that idiot ex-boyfriend of hers—Leo. The one who had said all those horrible things about her. About how she wasn't feminine enough. Wasn't woman enough to hold a man. And he'd just known he wanted to go, so that he could see her in all those pretty dresses and build up her confidence a little. If she needed it.

She didn't really want to go out with him. It was just to stop her father interfering again and trying to matchmake.

No. They were just friends. Even if his feelings for her were confusing. He loved Cara, yes—as he loved all of his friends. But he wasn't *in love* with her. At least, he didn't think so. It was just confusing because of how good they were together. How Cara reminded him of who he'd used to be.

So he'd agreed to go shopping with her. Find her a dress. Pretend to be her date at the ball. Maybe as long as they arrived together and were seen together by her father that would be enough. He could leave her to do her thing, and he would go and do his thing. Chat to whoever he knew there. The word about the ball had been spreading, and most of the paramedics who were going to be off duty had agreed to go. Why wouldn't they? They didn't very often get invited to a posh manor house and have the chance to get dressed up, all in the name of a good cause.

He was intrigued himself about the idea of going to Cara's family home. She didn't often talk about her childhood, and he wondered if, by going, he would understand her more. Cara had no airs and graces. She didn't expect to be treated differently because she was the daughter of an earl. She was just one of the guys to most people.

To him… She was that and more.

Tom gave Gage a bath and then read him a bedtime story. His son nodded off halfway through, no doubt exhausted by the football, so Tom left the book on his son's bedside cabinet so they could finish it off tomorrow. He switched off his lamp and crept back downstairs and sat in his lounge alone.

These were the moments he hated. When his son was asleep and it was late at night he felt more alone than he ever did at any other time.

He missed the simple act of sitting on the couch with someone, watching a movie, maybe having a nice glass of wine... He missed that feeling of connection, of having someone stroke his arm absently, or someone resting their head upon his shoulder. He hated going to bed alone. The bed seemed so big without anyone else in it. So empty.

Later Tom lay in his bed and stared up at the ceiling. He thought about Cara. About the way she'd looked playing football with his son. Her smile. Her laughter. The way the sun had caught the auburn tones of her hair, flashing fire. The way she'd looked at him, her eyes aglow, brightly gleaming with happiness. The way she'd made Gage laugh. The way she'd brightened his son's world.

And his.

What am I doing? I'm reading more into this than I should. She's just a friend. That's all she will ever be.

CHAPTER FOUR

'DAD, NO.' CARA had been hanging her things in her locker at work when her mobile phone had rung.

'Why not? Carenza can fit you in this weekend—she's already told me. All she needs are your measurements and she can whip you up something special for the ball.'

'I don't need a designer to make me a bespoke dress. I'll buy one from a shop. In fact, Tom is taking me out to find a dress later on today.'

Her father sounded doubtful. 'The *paramedic*?'

'Yes.'

A pause. 'You two an item, then?'

'Yes,' she lied, gritting her teeth, wishing she could be saying it with a smile, as if it were actually real.

'Oh, that's a shame. I'd rather told Henry

that you're single. He's bringing along his son Xander to meet you.'

She rolled her eyes. 'Well, Xander can say hello, but that's all he'll get from me. I'm with Tom.' She glanced around to make sure none of her crew mates from Green Watch were within hearing. There'd be no end of questions if they heard that. Not to mention the teasing she'd get. And if they found out it was fake…? It didn't bear thinking about.

Her father sighed. 'All right. But make sure the dress is something special. There's going to be a photographer, and I'm going to want official pictures of the only time my daughter wore a dress.'

'You're getting a photographer for *that*?'

'Not just for you, darling, don't worry. It's good publicity, what we're doing for the Werther family.'

'The Websters.'

'Ah, yes. Well, I've got to go. Do ring me and let me know when you've found something.'

'Fine.'

'And, darling?'

'Yes?'

'Just be careful. With Tom. A lot of men might be interested in you for reasons you don't suspect.'

Poor Dad. He thought lots of men were interested in her because she was a Lady! If only he knew that men didn't see her that way.

'He's not with me because of money, Dad.'

She sighed, wishing she could end this call, because it was becoming awful, and she hated lying to him, even if he was the one who had put her in this position in the first place.

'Just make sure—that's all.'

He said goodbye and ended the call.

Cara stood there, feeling an anger that boiled inside. It was so unfair! Her father was interfering in her life again. As she passed through the gym she gave the punchbag a thump, sending it swinging one way, then the other, before she headed to the canteen to make herself a drink before parade.

Reed and the others were already there, propping up the kitchen counters, slurping their tea from mugs.

'Morning, Cara,' said Reed.

'Morning.'

'Ready for another day?'

She nodded, smiled. 'Absolutely.' She filled the kettle with water, but before she could reach for a mug the station bell sounded. They had a shout.

They headed for the fire engine as Hodge

collected the call report. He met them as they dressed themselves in their uniforms.

'Male trapped in an industrial machine. That's all we have.'

Cara grimaced. That didn't sound good. But she switched herself into work mode and the fire engine, with sirens blaring, pulled out of the station, stopping the traffic, and went roaring in the direction of town.

As they passed the park that she and Tom and Gage had played football in she glanced out of the window, remembering the previous night. It had all been a little awkward after she'd asked Tom to accompany her to the ball as her date. Though she'd made it quite clear it was a fake date, she'd hated lying to Tom.

Why couldn't she just be brave enough to tell him the truth?

Because Victoria was an Amazonian goddess, that's why.

She'd distracted herself from her self-loathing and asked Gage to point out his favourite budgies in the aviary. She'd walked over to the birdcages, embarrassed to turn around and look at Tom. What on earth was he thinking? But eventually they had walked home, neither she nor Tom being overly chatty. Perhaps he was already regretting saying yes? Perhaps she was just being overly sensitive over this issue? Perhaps it was abundantly clear to Tom that this could never be anything but a fake date and so he wasn't worried at all? Because clearly he had no idea about her hidden feelings for him.

Which was just the way she wanted to keep it, thank you very much.

In a strange way she was looking forward to the dress-shopping tonight. Not because of the dresses. No. That part she was dreading. But spending time with Tom was always her favourite thing to do, and tonight he had a babysitter for Gage.

The fire engine sped through the traffic.

Hodge turned. 'Ambulance crew and rapid response are also on their way.'

Reed nudged her. 'Maybe lover-boy will be there.'

She glared at him.

They pulled into an industrialised area. Lots of lorries and vans loading up. A man in a bright yellow high vis jacket stood in the road, directing them to the place they needed to be, which was very much appreciated. He ran to greet them as they pulled up.

'Hi. I'm John—the manager. We've got one of our workers with his arm trapped in an industrial printing machine. It became jammed, and he was trying to clear the blockage, but got his arm trapped inside when it started up again. He's lost a lot of blood and is barely conscious.'

At that moment the rapid response vehicle turned up, with an ambulance and a police car following quickly behind. Tom got out, and he and the other medics were quickly filled in on what had happened.

John led them to the site of the accident.

'Has all this been turned off?' Hodge asked.

'Not all of it.'

'I want everything shut down whilst my crew are here. We don't need any further accidents as they try to help your man here. What's his name?'

'Pete.'

'Okay.' Hodge went over to the man, who was trapped in the machine up to his mid-upper arm and looking pale and weak. 'Pete? We're going to get you out of there, okay?' Hodge turned to John. 'Any chance you can get him a chair or something to sit on? If he passes out he's going to pull on that arm and maybe make his injury worse.'

John nodded and disappeared to get a chair.

Hodge took the opportunity to look at the machinery intently. To see where the arm was caught and if there was any easy way they could extract him.

'Okay, the machine's off Tom, do you want to take a look? It's safe for you to approach now.'

Hodge stepped back and Tom stepped forward. He'd already got an oxygen mask prepped and ready and he secured it to Pete's face.

Cara watched. The poor man! This was going to be a life-changing injury. He'd probably come to work this morning, thinking it was just going to be another ordinary day, but this had happened.

As Tom did his assessment, John came back with the chair.

'Where are your engineers?' asked Hodge. 'We're going to need people who can dismantle this machine, because I don't think you want us just cutting our way through it.'

'Er…no. We don't. I can call Carlos, but he's at home.'

'Anyone else?'

'The business down the road has the same machine as us. I can call them and ask if their engineer is on site? He'd get here quicker than Carlos would, as he doesn't have his own car and would have to rely on public transport.'

Hodge nodded. 'Call them.'

Tom was inserting a cannula for an IV into

Pete's arm. 'I'm giving you fluids and a pain-killer, okay?'

Pete nodded, his eyes barely open. Was he shutting down?

Tom grabbed his mobile. 'Control? I'm at the entrapment call. We need a doctor on site. This guy's going to want stronger painkillers than I can give him.'

'Confirmed. Heli-med en route.'

'Thank you, Control.' He turned to Hodge and the team. 'I can't do anything more until we get him clear of this machine.' He lowered his voice. 'Looking at the arm, I'm thinking we're looking at a possible amputation.'

Cara's heart sank. Pete was young. He had a wedding ring on his finger. She stepped forward. 'Pete? Can you open your eyes for me? Is there anyone we can call for you?'

Pete blinked, bleary-eyed, then nodded. With his free hand he pulled the oxygen mask away from his face. 'Sal. Call Sal. My wife.'

'Give me her number.'

Once he had, Tom put the oxygen mask back onto the man's face and checked his pressures and his pulse. 'He's going into shock.'

At that moment they heard running, and Cara turned to see a guy in dirty navy over-alls appear, puffing, out of breath, his eyes widening at the sight before him. 'You need an engineer?'

Hodge stepped up. 'Yes. We need this machine dismantled so we can free this man. What's your name?'

'Charlie.'

'Okay, Charlie. We need this done quick.'

'I've put on a tourniquet,' said Tom.

'Okay...' Charlie paused.

'Problem?' asked Cara.

'I'm just not very good with blood, and there's...um...a lot of it.' Charlie was starting to turn pale.

'Try not to look at that. Focus on what you need to do. I can help you.' Cara guided him forward with his toolbox and they set to work. They'd been working on the machine for maybe five minutes when a doctor arrived in an orange Heli-med jumpsuit.

'Can everyone just stand back so I can assess the patient, please?'

They all did, waiting and watching.

The doctor listened to the patient's chest, checked his pressures and examined the arm, which was still firmly trapped in the machine.

Pete was nearly completely unconscious.

'How long is it going to take to dismantle this machine?' he asked Charlie.

'Two hours, maybe?'

The doctor shook his head. 'The longer he stays trapped in that machine, the worse this is going to get. He's really struggling. His condition is deteriorating. I think we need to do an upper arm amputation and get him out. That arm is pretty mangled. I don't think there's any chance of saving it, and every second he's in there the more chance there is that infection will complicate matters.'

Tom nodded. 'Agreed.'

'Okay—let's do this.'

Charlie and the others backed off, and Tom and the Heli-med doctor set about preparing for amputation. They injected anaesthetic into Pete, so that he wouldn't feel anything, and began to manage his airway.

The doctor and Tom worked fast. Cara watched them. They moved as a perfect team. The doctor in charge, Tom assisting. This wasn't her first amputation, and she could remember being surprised at how fast someone could remove an arm or a leg. In her head, she'd always imagined it would take time. Carefully cutting through bone and muscle and sinew. Tying off blood vessels. Surely that should take hours? But, no. A couple of minutes and it was done.

Soon Pete was freed from the machine and lowered onto a trolley, where Tom and the other paramedics swarmed around him, getting his pressure back up and stabilising him for the trip to hospital via helicopter.

As Tom led Pete off on the trolley, Hodge got back to asking Charlie to open up the machine, so that they could still remove the mangled amputated arm.

Cara wished she'd had more of an opportunity to talk to Tom, but it had been all hands on deck. She would just have to wait to speak to him later that evening.

Tom knocked on Cara's door, trying not to feel as if he was picking her up for a date. Seriously, when had things changed? Because something had and he wasn't sure when. His feelings for her had crept up upon him, lurking like a shadow, always there but not always noticed. But now that he was *aware*, it was as if he couldn't stop noticing them.

He'd taken great care not to dress like a man going on a date. He wore dark jeans, a black tee, and a flannel shirt over the top. He'd not checked his hair before leaving, despite the almost unstoppable urge to comb it before leaving the house, because he needed this to just be another night out with a mate.

Dress-shopping.

Hmm...

He'd only ever gone dress-shopping before
with Victoria, and that had never gone well
at all. Commenting on the first two outfits
had been fine, but after that… He'd always
tried his hardest to not seem bored. Once,
when one of his friends had passed by, Victoria had let him off the hook and told him
he could go. And he had. But when he'd got
home she'd called him out on it.

Now, it was a memory that made him
cringe. He knew he should have cherished
every moment with her. But the truth of the
matter was that they'd often let each other
down. He wished he'd paid her more attention, but that particular dress-shopping out-
ing had been the day after a huge fight they'd
had, and the worse thing was he couldn't even
remember what the fight had been about.
Maybe work. By then Tom had been working long hours. Picking up extra shifts. Telling himself he was working hard to provide
for his family—which he was. He just wasn't
always there to enjoy the fruits of his labours.
Which Victoria would often complain about.

She'd said she felt like a single mother half
the time. And she'd been right. But it had
been easier to work than to argue, and he
hadn't wanted to argue. They'd had a lovely

baby boy together and he'd wanted he and Victoria to work *so much*!

Tom had had dreams of the future in which they were all together. Going on holidays. Getting close again. Finding the first flush of love that had brought them together in the early days. The feelings would still be there. They just needed rekindling. Somehow they'd both lost their way. Allowed the small things to become big things.

And he didn't ever want to make such a mistake again.

Maybe he wasn't cut out to be anyone's partner if he could screw up something that had once been so perfect? And Cara deserved someone who would put in one hundred percent. All the time. She had got him through his grief at the loss of his wife. Cara had become his rock and he couldn't lose her friendship. He needed her the way he needed air.

But he had to hold back. Not act on the strange feelings and thoughts about her that had often kept him awake at night lately. Wondering what she was doing. Who she might be with. There hadn't been a boyfriend since Leo, and he knew how much of a knock to her confidence Leo had given her. He wanted to be Cara's rock, too.

When she opened the door he smiled and

said hello, pushing back the reaction he really wanted to show.

She looked simply and stunningly beautiful. And Cara didn't know she was beautiful, which made her even more so. She was oblivious to how she made him feel. Her hair, usually up in a bun for work, was free and flowing. The orange-red flecks were catching the low evening light. The cool blue of her eyes, sparkling with happiness at seeing him, her friend, warmed his heart and stirred his blood. Deliberately, he stood back, casually turning around to look at the road, as if the traffic or the way the cars were parked were interesting, as he waited for her to grab her keys and phone.

She wore light blue skinny jeans, white trainers and a baggy crimson-coloured tee. Something Victoria would never have been caught wearing to go out. But the colour showed off Cara's pale, creamy skin to perfection, and as she locked her door the loose sleeve slipped down one arm to reveal a shoulder, smooth and toned. Her trapezius muscle, sculpted by many hours spent in the gym, showed the gorgeous slope of her neck.

'Ready?' she asked, turning to him.

'Yep.'

'I'm not. I figure I'm about to look a whole lot of stupid.'

She grimaced, clearly expecting him to laugh, so he gave a small chuckle and led the way to the car, fighting the urge to open the door for her, as a gentleman would. Instead, he walked round to the driver's side and let her get in the car by herself.

As they drove through the evening traffic, a song came on the radio. 'Ooh, I love this one!' she said, and turned up the volume and began singing, bopping away beside him.

She had a good voice. He loved listening to her sing. And the way she was clicking her fingers to the music and swaying beside him made him want to stop the car, throw off his seatbelt and take her in his arms and kiss her.

What the hell am I doing? I can't have these thoughts about Cara. It's not right.

He pushed those thoughts to the back of his skull and tried to concentrate on the traffic, praying for the song to be over. When it was he was able to relax a little more. He found a parking space near to the shopping centre, despite it being busy on a late-night shopping evening, and they got out, paid for their parking and began walking towards the shops.

He knew from experience that there were plenty of clothes shops there, but only one or two that sold the sort of dresses that Cara would be looking for.

'Let's go to Imagine first,' he suggested.

He remembered it from before, and knew it had a large range of dresses. He hoped that would mean she'd find one straight away and then this torture would be over.

'What's that?'

'It's a shop that sells posh dresses. Evening dresses. Ball gowns, wedding outfits—all of that.'

'How do you know about it?'

'It's right next door to the baby shop where we got Gage's pushchair and Moses basket.'

'OK, she said hesitantly.'

'You seem nervous.'

'I am. What if I look ridiculous in these dresses? I've got muscles, I'm broad-shouldered, with tattoos. I won't look right.'

He disagreed. 'You'll look amazing. We'll find you a beautiful dress.'

She bumped into him, nudging his arm with hers. 'Thanks for doing this. I really appreciate it.'

He smiled at her. 'No problem.'

Of course he was worried, too. Worried that he'd see her in each dress and fall for her just a little bit more with every one. He couldn't imagine her not looking good in anything she chose to wear. Cara could wear a potato sack if she wanted to and she'd look amazing. The fact that she didn't understand that blew him away. She was different from most women. She was happy to be without make-up, without having done her hair. She'd never had a manicure or a pedicure, or spent hours in a hairdressing salon, or a tanning booth, and she was *perfect*.

And although he'd kind of been looking forward to spending this time with Cara, now that it was imminent he found himself fearing the evening. He told himself to create distance, not to pay too much attention to how she looked. He'd look at her briefly, tell her she looked good in something, and then they could go home.

And yet... He didn't want to lie to her. He didn't want to dismiss her. But most of all he didn't want to ruin their friendship. Cara would know. Would sense if he was just giving her lip service. And Leo had ruined her self-esteem, so he was damned well going to tell her how gorgeous she looked and try not to give himself away.

Lip service... That just made him think about kissing her.

They headed into Imagine and he stood back as Cara took the lead, checking out the dresses hanging on the racks. There were dresses of all colours. Dazzling to the eye, some of them. He even saw one in bright neon orange, like a highlighter pen.

Cara looked at him. 'I didn't expect there'd be so many. How am I supposed to choose?'

'Pick ones that catch your eye and then try them on.'

'Hmm. I don't know...' She bit her lip, frowning.

'Can I help you?'

A very, tall, thin woman, dressed in a navy skirt suit and a cream silk blouse, approached them. She had glasses on a chain around her neck and wore an alarming amount of perfume.

'I need a dress. For a ball.'

The woman smiled. 'How lovely. Now, let me see...' She ran her eyes over Cara. 'You look to be about a twelve—am I right?'

'I guess...' Cara shrugged.

'You'll want something like...' The woman turned, casting her knowledgeable gaze over her stock. 'This. Or this.' She selected two dresses on hangers and presented them to Cara.

Cara turned to look at Tom, seeking his opinion.

He gave the usual male response and just shrugged.

'Why not try them on?' the woman suggested. 'The dressing room is over there.'

As Cara disappeared into the changing room Tom settled himself down in a chair and waited, pulling out his mobile phone to double-check that he didn't have any messages from the babysitter looking after Gage. The teenager next door often looked after Gage. She used those evenings to study for her exams, saying it was quieter in his house than in hers, where she had to share a bedroom with her younger sister.

There was no message, so he tried to sit back and relax. Eventually the door to the changing room opened and Cara stepped out wearing the first gown. He almost dropped his phone in shock and surprise.

The dress was a dark midnight-blue and on the hanger had just looked like any other swathe of fabric. Nothing special. But on Cara it looked...magical. As if she was wearing the night sky. It was asymmetrical. One-shouldered. Sweeping down across her chest to cradle and hold curves that he hadn't ever quite seen before. Cara was usually hidden under her firefighter uniform, or in baggy tees and jeans during her off hours. To see something this tight-fitting on her was...

He swallowed, trying to gather his thoughts, looking her up and down as if he were still thinking about what to say—and he was. He wanted to say *You look stunning. Gorgeous.* But he also didn't want her to realise just how affected he was at seeing her like this.

'You look lovely,' he managed, trying to sound normal.

Cara turned this way and that in front of the mirror. 'I don't know... I like the colour.'

The blue showed off her pale, creamy skin to perfection, and the tumble of her fiery hair, which she'd pulled to one side so she could look at the back of the dress, revealed to him her neck, her spine, the sweep of toned muscles beneath her skin.

This was a woman who could carry a grown man out of a burning building!

She had a waist. And curves that revealed hips that somehow pulled his gaze.

'I think I'd better try the other one on. What do you think?'

Tom nodded. 'Sure.'

He cleared his throat and let out a breath when she disappeared back inside the changing room.

What the hell was happening?

This was *Cara*. Cara! She was just his friend. She couldn't be anything else to him. He needed to stop having these thoughts about her. Hadn't she sworn off guys after Leo? Didn't Reed's daily attempts to wind her up remind her every day that guys could be idiots and not worth wasting her time on? Didn't she say that she was happy being single?

And she would never look at him in that way.

So he could never let her know how he was feeling.

It was probably a phase. It would pass! This was silly. He had nothing to worry about, surely? Just a phase...

The next dress was of ivory silk, and when Cara came out she looked like a Grecian goddess.

Tom felt that lump in his throat once again as he saw the draping silk emphasising her breasts, her trim waist, the swell of her hips.

'No, I can't wear this—it's practically indecent!'

Cara crossed her arms over her chest. Clearly it was impossible to wear a bra beneath the dress, and all he could think about were her nipples, which led to him thinking about what he could do to them...

He just nodded and said, 'Yeah, it is a bit… revealing.'

When she'd disappeared back into the changing room he let out a huff of air and got up and paced the shop, trying to make the part of his body below the waist feel a little more…relaxed. He shook out his legs, tried to slow his breathing, and couldn't remember if clothes-shopping with Victoria had ever been like this.

He didn't think so.

When Cara came back out, dressed in her baggy tee once again, he smiled and sighed a sigh of relief.

'Maybe we should try somewhere else?' she said.

'Sure…er…there's another dress shop at the end of this road.'

The besuited woman behind the till smiled as they left, and Tom was glad of the fresh air and the cool evening wind that was beginning to blow. It had got rather hot in Imagine. And now he understood why the shop was called what it was…because his mind had certainly imagined all sorts of scenarios.

The next boutique dress shop was smaller than Imagine, but the assistant was just as helpful. She helped pick out three dresses for Cara. The first was fire-engine-red, which

Cara loved, but she really wasn't too keen on the choker neckline as she thought it made her shoulders look too broad. The second was an ombre dress, in seaweed-green, its colour changing to a Mediterranean-blue at the neck, but Cara said she felt like a fairy in it. The third dress was an iridescent black that shimmered and draped her body like an oil slick.

'What do you think?' She turned in front of him, and as she did so revealed a very high split that went almost to the top of her thigh.

He pressed his lips together hard, wondering just what it was that he'd done wrong in this life that he was being punished in such a manner?

Cara grabbed at the fabric to hold it together. 'It's too revealing, huh?' she said, blushing, looking awkward. 'I'll go and change.'

'No. It's…um…lovely.'

Lovely? *Lovely?* Couldn't he think of another adjective? Had he turned into his father? That was what his dad said to things. To a nicely brewed cup of tea. To a nice slice of cake. To a comfy chair.

Cara was beyond *lovely* in these dresses.

'I feel exposed.' She turned to the assistant. 'Have you got anything that doesn't reveal ninety percent of my skin? It's just not me.'

'Let me think…' The assistant turned to survey the shop and then snapped her fingers. 'Do you know? I just might have something in the back. Bear with me for a moment.'

Cara nodded, still clutching the split in the dress to cover her leg.

Tom wished he had a drink to hand. His mouth was so dry! Cara wasn't tall by any means. She was a whole head shorter than him. But that split made it look as if her beautifully toned legs went on for days…

When the assistant came back out, with a dress hidden inside a cover, he found himself hoping and praying that this one would not make him feel as if he wanted to ravish his best friend, as all the others had done.

His right leg was twitching, his foot rapidly tapping the floor in a staccato rhythm as his nerves increased, while he waited for Cara to come out.

When she did he stood up, a smile breaking over his face at the sight of the smile on hers, and he knew she'd found a dress she was happy with.

It was long-sleeved, high-necked and stylishly draped, in a beautiful gold colour. It showed no cleavage. It had no leg-split. But the diamanté and sequins that were sewn into the dress in their thousands made her look like a starburst.

'You look…gorgeous,' he said, his breath almost taken from him. She'd looked amazing in everything, but this… This dress made her happy, and that was what counted the most.

She blushed at his praise. 'You think? It's got this at the back, but…'

She turned, and he saw that the dress exposed most of her back, all the way down to the top of her bottom. The gentle swell of her butt cheeks caused the golden shine to blind his eyes. It was just her back, but it seemed to be the most erotic thing he had ever seen and his body stirred in reaction to her.

Tom sat down. Awkwardly. 'It's amazing. What do you think?' He cleared his throat again, trying to regain control of his body. Who knew it could do so many things involuntarily?

'I like it. You don't think the back's too much?' She turned again, giving him another glance of her skin, the curve of her waist…

'No, it's…perfect.'

'It's a good price, too.' Cara admired her reflection in the mirror for a while, before turning to the assistant and saying, 'I'll take it.'

'Fabulous!' the assistant said.

Tom smiled, but inwardly he was telling

himself, *Okay, so she's going to wear that dress. Keep your hands high, and when you get to the party you don't have to stay close. You'll have done your part. You'll have warned off anybody wanting to ask her out. You'll just have to get through one dance with her and that will be—what? Two minutes long? Three, tops? Then it'll be a drive home, a quick peck on the cheek to say goodnight and it'll all be over. Easy, right?*

Then they could go back to normal, and eventually the memory of her in that dress would fade, and they could just be mates. That was all he wanted. He didn't want to get involved with anyone again. Not really. It was horrible when you lost someone, and he didn't want to lose Cara if this all went wrong.

No. He could behave himself. He was a gentleman.

And that was what Cara deserved.

CHAPTER FIVE

CARA HAD A day off. And she was determined to use it to get stuff done that she couldn't when she was at work. There was a wonky cupboard door in her kitchen that needed repairing, and a pipe that needed replacing under the sink. She'd bought the parts ages ago but had just never got round to it. So she pulled up some music on her phone and began clearing out all the cleaning essentials she kept under her sink so she could expose the pipe.

As she worked, her mind kept drifting to the previous evening, dress-shopping with Tom.

It had been crazy. Each of those first few dresses had made her feel as if she was naked in front of Tom, and that had done some incredible things to her insides! She'd almost not come out of the changing rooms a couple of times, but she had forced herself, curious as to how he might react. He was her friend, but he was also a red-blooded male, and some of those dresses had been...risqué.

He had looked a little as if he didn't know where to look, and that had embarrassed her to begin with. Clearly he'd believed she looked ridiculous in those exquisitely feminine dresses. Dresses meant for women like Victoria. With long, lean limbs and a flat stomach. Women who were fully in touch with their femininity.

Cara wasn't a girly girl. She didn't get the whole thing about how to be a stereotypical woman, interested in handbags and nails and having her hair done every six weeks. She preferred trimming her own hair in front of her bathroom mirror. Handbags were useless if you had enough pockets. And fake nails? How did anybody do anything with those long claws on? And she bit her nails more than she decorated them.

I was kidding myself if I thought Tom might find me attractive in those dresses.

Cara wasn't a woman who used her womanly wiles. She'd never needed other men to notice her. Tom was the only one who was important. The only one who mattered. And it had mattered what he thought of the dresses—especially when she'd felt so uncomfortable in them.

Except for that last one. The gold one. It had covered all the essentials. The shoulders she thought were too broad, the arms that were probably a little too muscly, the cleavage that was too small anyway and the thighs that were thick with muscle and should only be revealed, if at all, to a physiotherapist or a doctor.

She'd felt confident in the gold dress. As if she could carry it off. Because the evening was going to be difficult enough as it was—what with her father being as annoying as always and it being her mother's birthday and the fact that it would be a fake date with Tom. It all made her feel uncomfortable, and she needed a dress to make her feel okay.

Cara would love it to be a real date, but fake would do. They'd walk in together as a couple. Surprise Green Watch. But she would explain it to them later, when the party was over. For a few hours she would pretend and be happy.

Maybe they'd walk in arm in arm? That would be nice. Tom would be attentive and at her side all night, with his arm around her protectively, his hand resting on her hip, her body pressed against his. She would be able to get through the evening like that, no problem. Her heart would probably be racing through it all, but it would be worth it.

And then Tom would take her home and escort her to her door and plant a kiss upon her cheek before saying goodnight. And then she would have to fight the urge to ask him in for coffee, knowing that she wouldn't want the night to end. Because when it did they would go back to being normal friends. Which was great. But when the heart wanted more...

I can't make him love me. I can't make him see me as something else.

Plus, there was Gage to think about. That little boy had been through so much, and although she loved him to bits, loved spending time with him and making him laugh, she would never be able to replace his mother and Tom wasn't the kind of man who entered relationships lightly. He'd only ever been in one and that had been with Victoria. He was no gigolo, no fly-by-night, no *wham, bam, thank you, ma'am* kind of guy. Tom only did serious relationships.

Maybe she could talk to him about that? Ask him gently, as his friend, if he'd ever considered dating again? Test the waters?

What would it feel like to see him with someone else?

She didn't like that thought.

It would be tragic and hurtful. Make her sad.

The pipe came free and some water splashed down upon her, making her splutter and wipe off the excess. She put the new pipe in place and began to fasten it on, making sure there were no leaks by running the tap above.

It worked perfectly.

If only people could be fixed so easily.

'She's dislocated her elbow,' Tom said to the father cradling his daughter in his lap.

The patient was a young child, only two years of age, and the elbow had been dislocated by her father spinning her around in the garden by the arms. The pulling mechanism of the injury was classic.

'I did it. I feel so guilty. Does she need to go to hospital?'

Tom shook his head. 'No. I can fix it here. It's usually an easy fix, but when I put the elbow back into place she might cry out for a moment. Hey, Lacey? I'm going to fix your arm, okay?'

Lacey snuggled further into her father.

That was okay. Tom was a stranger to her and she was in discomfort—it was to be expected. Tom rolled up the girl's sleeve and held her elbow in his right hand, supporting it so that when he performed the manoeuvre he would be able to feel the elbow pop back into place. He took Lacey's hand in his left hand, as if they were shaking hands, then turned her palm upwards towards the ceiling, straightened the arm, pulling outwards, and felt the elbow snap back into place as he folded her arm at the antecubital fold.

Lacey cried out at the click, but when Tom offered her a tongue depressor to hold and she used her left arm for the first time since the dislocation a smile crept onto her face.

'See? All fixed.'

'It's done?' Lacey's dad asked. 'That's amazing.'

'It's one of my favourite things to do.' Tom smiled. 'Make a patient better quickly. If only all my jobs were this easy.'

'Well, I can't thank you enough. I really thought I'd broken her arm.'

'If I could take away your guilt I'd do so, believe me.' Tom smiled at Lacey. 'Maybe Daddy will find a nice treat for you because you were so brave?'

'Ice cream!' Lacey said, looking up at her dad.

Tom laughed, just as his personal mobile rang. He stood up to pull it from his trouser pocket and frowned. Gage's pre-school was calling him.

'Excuse me. I need to take this.' He turned away and walked out into the hall for some privacy. 'Hello?'

'Hello, is that Gage's dad?' asked a female voice.

'Yes.'

'I'm sorry to call you. This is Fiona Goddard from Sunflowers Pre-School.'

'Yes?'

'It seems that Gage isn't feeling very well. He's complaining of a tummy ache and he's not quite himself. Would you be able to pick him up?'

Tom sighed. 'I'm at work.'

'I understand. But we can't keep him here if he's not feeling well. Is there any way you could come? Or a family member who could?'

His mind raced. Who could he call? Who would Gage feel comfortable with? He knew immediately.

'I'll need to check with a friend. I'll call you back and let you know.'

'Thanks.'

He ended the call and dialled Cara's number. When she answered he heard music playing in the background. 'Hey, it's me. Where are you? Sounds like you're in a disco.'

'You're right. It's 1986 in here.' The music went down a notch. 'I'm fixing a kitchen cupboard—what can I do you for?'

He sighed. 'I realise this is an imposition, but I've just been called by Gage's nursery. He's not feeling well and they want him to be collected, and—'

'I'm on my way. Let them know I'm coming. I'll take him back to yours. Is the spare key still in that fake plant pot?'

This was why she was so great. There weren't many people he could rely on like this. He could have called his parents, but they didn't have their own car now and they lived nearly an hour away—probably more if he took into account how long it would take them to get to Gage's nursery by public transport. Cara knew where it was, and she was close, and he trusted her with his son.

'It is—and thanks. I know this is your day off.'

'I've already done what I set out to do today. All I had planned after this was to sit and watch a movie. I can do that with Gage. What's wrong with him?'

'Tummy ache.'

'Ah… I can deal with that—no problem.'

'Thanks, Cara. I don't know what I'd do without you.'

There was a brief silence. 'You'd do fine.'

'I doubt it.'

He really did. He honestly thought that he'd still be wallowing in grief and guilt right now if it hadn't been for her. She brightened his day…gave him the belief that he could do anything he wanted if he just put his mind to it. She was his cheerleader, his rock, and soon she was going to be his date for a ball. A fake date, but he was looking forward to seeing her in that dress again. Just to reassure himself that she had looked that amazing and it wasn't just his imagination that had made the whole thing up. He was going to feel honoured to walk into Higham Manor with Cara on his arm.

'We'll be fine. What's the safe word?'

The nursery had a safe word system, so if a parent couldn't collect a child any other adult would have to use the parent-created safe word before they'd be allowed to walk off with someone else's child.

He grimaced. 'Don't laugh, okay?'

'I promise.'

'It's banana.'

He heard a muffled laugh. 'Banana?' She was trying to sound serious. 'Interesting…'

'I was eating one when I filled in the form. I never thought I'd actually have to use it.'

'Sounds legit. Okay. See you later.'

She rang off and he stood there for a moment, just staring at his phone, before dialling the nursery to let them know that Cara would be collecting Gage.

When he'd put his phone back in his pocket he went into the living room and smiled at Lacey and her father. Lacey was now sitting on the floor, playing with a toy car, using the arm he'd just fixed.

'See how quickly they forget that they used to hurt?'

'You're a miracle worker,' Lacey's father said.

But Tom didn't think so.

Cara was the miracle worker—not him. She'd got him smiling again, laughing again, when after Victoria's death he'd never thought that would ever be possible.

Cara set Gage down by the front door whilst she surreptitiously located the spare key and opened the front door, ushering the little boy into the living room.

Gage sat on the couch, looking solemn.

She knelt in front of him, smiling warmly. 'Okay. Operation Tummy Ache. What are we talking about here? Does it just hurt? Or are we going to need a bucket?'

Gage smiled. 'It just hurts.'

'Show me where.'

He pointed to the middle of his abdomen.

'Okay. I think I may need to operate. Lie back and be brave. I promise to be quick.'

Gage giggled and lay back. He didn't look comfy, so she grabbed a cushion and put it under his head, and then dragged a holey crocheted throw from off the back of the couch and draped it over his little form.

'TV?'

He nodded.

'What do you fancy watching? Politics? The news? Antique-hunting?'

'Cartoons.'

'I think I can manage that.' She turned and pointed the remote at the screen. It came to life and she brought up the menu to find the channel that showed cartoons all day. 'I prescribe three cartoons. Then I'll read you a story and maybe you can try and sleep, okay?'

'Okay.'

'Do you want a drink?'

'Milk!'

'With a bad tummy? Hmm…how about some juice?'

'Okay.'

She laid the back of her hand against his forehead. He didn't feel hot, which was good.

It was probably just a bug, if it was anything at all.

'You watch TV while I make the drinks, and then I'll come back here and sit with you—how about that?'

He nodded.

Cara gave his hair a ruffle, then went to get their drinks. It didn't take long, and she was soon back on the couch with Gage, watching a weird cartoon that she thought was awful but pretended to like. Her gaze kept falling upon the picture of Victoria on the mantelpiece, and all she could think of was how it ought to be Victoria getting the chance to sit with her son. She'd be so proud of him. He was growing into a lovely boy, and Tom was doing remarkable things with him, raising him not to feel out of place because he didn't have a mum, like the other kids did.

What would Victoria do if she was here? Stroke Gage's hair? Keep an eye on him at a distance whilst she got on with some housework? Put Gage in his bedroom?

Tom's wife looked down at Cara on the couch and seemed to say *Well, I'm not there, so do the best for my son. I'm trusting you with him. I'm trusting you with* them.

Cara had become Victoria's friend, however brief that friendship had been. What would she think if she could know that Cara had secret thoughts about her husband? Had *fantasies*? She'd be appalled, that was what. She wouldn't want Cara to be anywhere near them. She'd feel betrayed.

Guilt swallowed her and she looked down at Gage. What was she doing, having these thoughts about Tom?

I can't! I shouldn't!

She sipped at her tea, and when they reached the end of the third cartoon she swallowed hard and switched off the television.

'Aww!' Gage protested.

'Storytime, bucko. I can't have you getting square eyes as well as a tummy ache.'

Gage touched his face. 'Are my eyes going square?'

She laughed. 'It's just a saying. Your eyes don't actually change shape.'

'That would look funny.'

'It would. So! Storytime...' Underneath the coffee table was a small pile of children's books. She scooped them out and presented them to him like a magician, saying, 'Pick a card...any card.'

Gage pursed his lips, then pointed at a book.

'Excellent choice, *monsieur.*' She put the others down and then sat back on the couch, draping some of the crocheted throw over her own legs, and settled down and began to read.

As she spoke she held the book to one side, so that Gage could see the pictures. He lay there, listening intently, his eyes growing heavy, until eventually, about three pages from the end, he nodded off and his little cherub face grew soft in repose.

Cara closed the book with a smile and snuggled down on the couch next to him, watching him sleep, thinking how wonderful it would be to have her own little family. What she wouldn't give to have a little boy like Gage. He was perfect and she loved him a lot.

The warmth of the blanket and the softness of the couch soon had their effect on Cara, too, and she fell fast asleep, the book slipping from her grasp and falling to the floor.

Tom's shift finished at midday. He'd been on since seven a.m., just five hours, but when he'd told Control he had a sick little boy at home they'd told him to go home early, which he was really grateful for. Obviously they knew he was a single dad, and they had been brilliant at accommodating him when life got tough. Like today.

He knew he could have stayed, finished

his shift in its entirety, but he didn't want to take advantage of Cara's good nature. Despite her protest that picking up Gage from pre-school was just fine by her, he was very much aware that this was a precious day off for Cara and he'd hijacked it. With his family and his problems. That was why he was happy to help Cara out with this ball thing… being her fake boyfriend. Anything to make her life a little bit easier, the way she did so often for him.

Not sure if Gage would be sleeping, he quietly turned his key in the lock and opened the door. The house was pretty silent. Fighting the urge to call out either of their names, he tiptoed down the hall after discarding his work shoes and popped his head through the living room door.

And felt his heart melt with adoration.

Cara and Gage were both fast asleep on the couch, covered in the raggedy blanket that Victoria had made in an attempt to learn something new. It had huge gaps between the stitches. Some of the squares were smaller than the others. The colours clashed. But it had been made with love, and after his wife had died he'd not been able to bear parting with something that had been made by her hand.

For a moment he stood there, gazing down

adoringly at both of them. He grabbed his mobile phone, opened up the camera app and took a photo.

The sound of the camera woke Cara. She blinked her eyes open, then sat up in shock, half of her hair squashed to the side of her head by the cushion she'd been sleeping on. Immediately she blushed, then looked down at Gage to check that he was all right.

'Oh, my gosh. I'm so sorry. I must have fallen asleep.'

He smiled at her. 'You did,' he whispered, turning the phone so she could see the picture.

'I must have been more tired than I thought.' She cocked her head to one side and ruffled her hair. 'Do I really look like that when I'm asleep?'

'Apparently.'

'I hope I didn't drool.' She wiped her mouth.

Tom used the zoom function on the photo. 'No drool. How's the patient?'

She smiled. 'Good. Centralised tummy pain, no temperature, no vomiting. He's kept down his juice and...' she checked the time '... I was going to see if he wanted some toast for his lunch.'

'You go. I'll do all that. Enjoy what's left of your day off.'

'Oh, it's no problem. I've enjoyed myself.'

'I can see that.' He grinned. 'I'm going to take this one up to bed. Give me a minute.' Gently, he scooped up his son, who barely woke except to snuggle in closer to his dad's chest as Tom carried him up the stairs.

This was what being a parent was all about, Tom thought. These moments when your kid snuggled into you. When he was dopey with sleep. When he reached for you to provide comfort and love.

'Hello, Daddy.' Gage mumbled.

'Hey, you. How are you feeling?'

His son nuzzled his nose into Tom's top. 'Fine.'

'That must be because you had a good nurse looking after you, hey?'

Gage smiled. 'Can she stay?'

Tom felt an ache in his heart, but he was almost at the top of the stairs and heading towards Gage's bedroom, so he felt it was safe to whisper. 'Not today.'

'You could ask her for a sleepover.'

'Maybe.'

'It doesn't matter that it's not night-time. We had a pretend sleepover at pre-school last week. We told stories and had hot chocolate.'

'Sounds good.'

'She could sleep in my bed with me.'

He smiled, loving the innocence of a three-year-old boy. 'Well, maybe when you're better.'

'And we could look after Cara when she has a tummy ache.'

'We could.'

'You make people feel better all the time, Daddy.'

Tom laid his son in bed and pulled his football duvet cover over him. 'Rest and I'll bring you up something to eat. What do you fancy?'

'Hot dogs.'

'Let's start with something plain, huh? How about some delicious toast?'

Gage nodded from beneath the quilt.

'Okay. Back in a bit.'

Tom trotted downstairs to find Cara folding the crocheted blanket and draping it into position on the back of the couch.

'I remember Victoria making this,' she said, stroking the blanket.

He nodded. 'Me too.'

'She swore a lot.' Cara looked up at him and smiled.

'She was never very good at making things. Except Gage. He's pretty perfect.'

'Well, you had something to do with that, too.'

'I'm going to make him some toast. Fancy

staying for lunch?' he asked, feeling nervous that she'd say no. Feeling nervous that she'd say yes.

'I'd love to.'

The next day, Cara was four hours into her shift when a call came through for a cyclist versus bus. She clambered into her uniform with the rest of Green Watch and got into the appliance, and with sirens and lights blazing they made their way through town, towards the co-ordinates they'd been given.

It was a busy high street, and the traffic had come to a standstill because of the accident. Reed, who was driving, had to sound his horn to get people to move, so they could make their way through. Eventually they got as close as they could and Cara clambered from the truck, hearing sirens in the distance as police and ambulances made their way to the accident.

Hodge led the way towards the bus, which was stopped at a weird angle just past its last stop. It must have been pulling away after picking up its latest passengers and collided with the cyclist. But…where was the cyclist?

Cara got down on her hands and knees and saw a bike and a body beneath the bus. The front wheel of the vehicle was half resting on the cyclist's leg. The cyclist was crying quietly.

'Let's get some stabilisers!' Cara called out, lying down on her stomach and trying to make eye contact with the cyclist, who was just out of reach. Otherwise Cara would have reached for her hand.

As the others placed wheel chocks down, to stabilise the vehicle, Tom arrived alongside her.

'What have we got?'

'Leg entrapment, as far as I can see, but I have no idea if the wheel went over her chest or her pelvis first.'

'She's conscious?'

Cara nodded. 'We'll need to use inflation devices to lift the bus, so that we can pull her out from under there.'

'Okay. I'll get painkillers ready for injection.'

Cara looked back at the cyclist. 'We're going to get you out of there soon, okay? What's your name, love?'

'Penny.'

'Okay, Penny. That's it…just focus on me. There's going to be a lot going on around you, but I don't want you to worry about that. Just keep talking to me. What hurts the most?'

'I—I don't know. My stomach…'

That didn't bode well.

'Can you feel your legs?'

Penny paused, then shook her head, terrified. 'No!'

'Okay. I need you to stay calm. You may just have spinal shock. We won't know until we get you to the hospital, so stay positive.'

Penny sniffed and nodded. 'Okay...'

'Where were you going today, Penny?'

'The bank and the p-post office.'

'Paying bills or taking money out?'

'Taking out. For a h-holiday.'

'Fantastic! Where are you thinking of going?'

As Cara kept Penny occupied the rest of Green Watch did their thing, finding the correct placement for the inflation devices that would slowly lift the bus from the patient.

'Crete. I have family over there.'

'Parents?'

Penny nodded. 'I haven't seen them since before the pandemic. I've been saving so I can go. Will I be able to go now?'

'Maybe not tomorrow, but let's say yes—you're going to go to Crete.'

'I'm going to go...' Penny looked about her. 'What's your name?'

'Cara.'

'That's pretty. I knew a Cara once...when I was little.'

'Yeah?'

'She went to my school. It was a boarding school. Monrose...'

Cara frowned. She'd gone to Monrose! Wait... Penny... Was this...?

'Penelope Moorcroft?'

Penny blinked. 'Cara Maddox? *Lady* Cara Maddox?'

Cara smiled. 'It's me.'

'But...you're a fireman. I mean, a fire p-person.'

She nodded. 'Yes, I am. I never expected to meet you again like this.'

'You were such a nice girl at school. I remember being f-frightened on my first day, and you took me to the nurse when I got a headache.'

Cara remembered. 'Looks like I'm going to be delivering you to medics again. Maybe we should stop meeting like this?'

'Maybe.' Penny gave a small laugh. Then, 'Why can't I feel my legs, Cara?'

Cara kept her voice calm. 'The doctors won't know until they scan you.'

'Am I going to die? I'm getting cold...'

'She's in shock,' whispered Tom. 'We need to get her out fast.'

'I know.'

'Why are you whispering?' Penny called.

'We're not. Just working out how best to get you out quick.'

'Ideally, I'd like to get some pain meds into her before we lift this bus,' said Tom. 'Let me shimmy under there. You've secured the vehicle—it won't move.'

'Tom—'

'If we lift this bus from her leg it's going to be agony. She could have compartment syndrome and all the toxins will go straight to her heart, putting her into arrest. I need to be under there with her.'

'I can't put you at risk, Tom.'

'I won't be.' He smiled. 'Not with Green Watch's finest looking after me.'

'I'll need to check with Hodge,' Cara told him. 'Penny? I'll be back in just a second.'

But as she got up and turned her back she saw a movement out of the corner of her eye, and when she turned back she saw the toe ends of Tom's boots as he shimmied underneath the bus, dragging his kitbag with him.

'Tom!'

She couldn't believe he'd done that! It was dangerous. If anyone should have gone underneath, it should have been her. Now Tom could get hurt, and the idea of that happening made her feel sick. Sweat bloomed in her armpits and down her back.

'Hodge! Tom's gone under.' Cara hated hearing the panic in her voice. The fear.

Hodge got down on his hands and knees and spoke to Tom. 'What are you playing at?'

'Keeping my patient alive and pain-free!' Tom's disembodied voice came back.

Cara lay flat on her stomach again, to see what was happening, but Tom was in front of the patient now and she couldn't see what was going on.

'When you get those pain meds on board, you come right back out—you hear me, Tom Roker?'

'Yes, ma'am.'

She cursed silently and looked over at Reed and Garrett and beyond him David Garcia. They all gave a thumbs-up. They were ready to inflate the blocks.

'We're all set out here. Are you done yet, Tom?'

'Nearly... Okay, I'm coming back out.'

Her heart began to slow down as more and more of Tom's body came safely out from underneath the bus. His uniform had oil on it, and he was scuffed and dirty, but he gave her a grin that stopped her from being angry. *He was safe*. That was what mattered.

She turned her attention back to her patient. 'Penny? We're going to inflate now, and we'll have you out in a jiffy.'

'She won't answer you. I've given her some ketamine, so she's woozy.'

'Okay, let's get this bus off this poor woman,' said Hodge, signalling the lift to begin.

The machines started up, slowly inflating the concertinaed blocks that had been placed at strategic points underneath the bus. It seemed to take ages, but eventually the bus was lifted clear of Penny's legs.

Both Tom, Hodge and Cara helped pull her out, and once she was clear Tom began working on her quickly, alongside the other paramedics who swarmed in from nowhere, along with a doctor who must have arrived in a helicopter, judging by his bright orange jumpsuit.

Cara, Garrett and Reed deflated the blocks and the bus sank back down to the road.

The police had created a barrier around the accident site and were marking the road and taking witness statements. Tom and the others got Penny onto a backboard and whisked her over to an ambulance, so she could be kept warm whilst the doctor oversaw her care.

Cara looked at the giant wheels of the bus and imagined the weight of that vehicle going over a pelvis or a spine. Unless Penny was extremely lucky, her outlook might not be all that great. The likelihood was that there was going to be a lot of surgery and physio-therapy in the months to come.

As the helicopter rose into the air with its patient onboard Cara found Tom, grabbing his arm and making him turn forcibly. 'Don't you *ever* do that to me *ever* again!'

CHAPTER SIX

HE'D NEVER SEEN such anger and fear in her eyes. Cara had been *furious* with him. It was an emotion he wasn't used to from her. In the entire time he'd known her she'd only ever been calm, funny, happy, supportive and caring.

But anger? And fear?

He'd tried to apologise, but he really felt he'd done the right thing. If he hadn't, Penny would have been in a whole world of pain when that bus had been lifted.

Once they'd got her out, they'd discovered she had an unstable pelvic fracture, two broken femurs and a suspected lower spine fracture. That was a lot of injury to one body, and without pain meds it would have been horrific. Penny had been numb from the waist down, but that might have been shock, or her mind protecting her from her horrific injury, but once the adrenaline had worn off she would have felt everything if he hadn't gone under the bus.

It had been safe. The bus had been stabilised. There had been no other traffic flowing around them and he had made a judgement call.

But Cara's response had him flummoxed. Was it more than the response of just a friend? Or was he trying to read too much into this?

Now, as he drove them both to the shopping centre once again, to help Cara find shoes to go with her golden dress, Cara sat in silence, staring out of the window. It was an awkward silence and one he wasn't sure how to navigate. He didn't want to make things worse, but he really hated not being able to talk to her. And having her angry with him like this made him feel repentant.

'So…are we not going to talk to each other this evening or…?' He let the question hang.

Cara sighed. 'We can talk. So long as you admit you were reckless.'

'I don't think I was.'

She glared at him. 'Silence it is, then.'

'I'm sorry if I scared you by going under that bus. That wasn't my intention.'

'We hadn't had confirmation it was fully stable, Tom! What if the bus had come down on you? You could have been hurt! You could have been injured. Badly. And then what would Gage do, huh? Without his mother *and* his father?'

Tom got what she was saying, but he was also hearing what she *wasn't* saying out loud. Clearly she was worried about how his getting hurt would affect *her.* Wasn't she? And if she was, what did *that* mean? And if it did mean something…if it did mean that Cara had feelings for him that went beyond friendship, then…

No. He was being ridiculous. She was probably worried that if he got hurt she'd have to rescue him too. That she'd have to take on too much with Gage, or something.

He thought for a moment, trying to think of ways to lighten the mood and take his mind off his quandary. 'Well, I don't have much experience in shoe-shopping with women, but from what I do know it's meant to be a happy experience.'

'Maybe. You could always drop me off. I can go alone.'

'Cara, please. I'm trying to say sorry, here.'

She looked at him. 'You scared me, Tom. Going under that bus like that. It made me feel helpless. That if something were to happen to you I wouldn't be able to protect you.'

So he was right, then. She was just worried

about having to rescue two people instead of one. It was nothing to do with her having feelings for him. It was a realisation that made him feel glum.

'I was fine.'

'Luckily. Aren't you guys taught not to rush to a patient without checking the scene is safe for you first?'

He nodded. 'It *was* safe. You'd stabilised the bus.'

'But I needed to check with Hodge first. He was in charge of everyone's safety at the scene—not you.'

'I get it. And I'm sorry I scared you.'

He liked it that she cared so much. Just not in the way that he'd hoped for. But he was her friend—maybe her best friend. Either way, it felt good to know that someone cared and worried about him. His parents did, obviously, but it wasn't the same as having Cara care. Knowing that she was thinking about him, worrying about him... What had she said? It had made her feel *helpless*.

He reached over and laid his hand on hers. Her skin was smooth and warm. 'I'm sorry,' he said, and he meant it. It wasn't a half-baked apology just to stop the awkward silence. He really meant it. He didn't want her to worry about him. He knew how it felt to worry over someone you couldn't help. And that help-less feeling…? He was intimately aware of it. 'I promise to never make you feel that way again.'

'And you'll wait for me to say something is safe before you go charging in on your white horse?'

'I will wait.'

She gave him a small smile. 'Good. I hate being angry with you. I'm not used to it.'

'Me neither.'

He drove, still holding her hand, enjoying the way it made him feel, trying not to read too much into it but not keen on letting go, either. If he could hold Cara's hand for ev-ermore, he would. But it seemed they were doomed to be nothing more than friends.

'How's Gage today?' she asked.

'His normal self, thankfully. Back at pre-school.'

'I'm glad.'

'He wanted to know if you were going to come round again soon, to teach him how to do keepy-uppies?'

'Can't you show him?'

'I can't do them.' He squeezed her hand. 'And he wants to learn from the best.'

She laughed. 'Tell him I'll see him at the weekend.'

He had to slow his car as they reached the traffic lights near to the shopping centre, and he had to let go of her hand to operate the gears. His own hand suddenly felt so empty, and he yearned to reach out and take her hand again. But he knew that would seem odd. That was a boyfriend gesture, and he was not Cara's boyfriend.

The moment was over.

They were back to being best friends again.

And even though he feared it would never seem enough, he was willing to take it.

Some of Cara was better than no Cara at all.

The first shoe shop had a display of trainers at the front, and Cara *oohed* and went over to take a look at a black pair that had a flash of neon green near the toe.

'These are awesome,' she said, taking in the neat construction, the multi-coloured laces and the supportive reinforced heel.

But Tom took them from her hands and placed them back down on the stand. 'We're here for something that will match your dress, and I don't think that these will do.'

'Not fair...' she protested, as he led her towards the other side of the shop, where there was a more dazzling array of strappy shoes with heels.

Cara gazed at them, feeling utterly lost. What was she meant to do? She knew nothing about shoes. Was she meant to wear gold shoes with a gold dress? Did they have to match? Or could she wear a neutral colour? A nude? Something contrasting?

'I fail miserably at being a girl.'

Tom laughed. 'You're perfect.'

'Am I? What do I know about shoes? Apart from the fact that they go on your feet and that I'll always choose comfort over style.'

'Last I heard, being a girl didn't mean passing any shoe exams.'

She picked up a pair of pale pink ballet shoes. 'Thankfully. I'd definitely fail. Are these any good?'

Tom shook his head. 'Not with that dress. That dress is…something special. You want a shoe that reflects that.' He picked up a high-heeled strappy shoe in gold. 'What about these?'

Cara turned the shoe over in her hands. 'How are you supposed to walk in these?'

'Gracefully?'

She laughed. 'Have you ever seen me in a heel?'

He shook his head. 'No. I don't think I ever have.'

'Well, there's a reason for that. I look like a toddler who's just found her mummy's shoes. I either look ridiculous or I fall over. These look like they'd break my ankles.'

'Try them on and see.'

'Let's leave them in reserve. What else is there?'

She cast her gaze over the racks. There seemed to be shoes in most colours. There was a lot of black, but she felt pretty sure a black shoe wouldn't look great with the gold dress. She saw a pair that had a small chunky heel. A kitten heel? Was that what it was called? Bubblegum-pink and kind of cute.

'These?'

Tom shrugged. 'Try it on.'

She sat down, pulled off one trainer and a short sock and slid her foot into the shoe. She wondered if she was meant to have painted her toenails. Did Tom think she had ugly feet?

Cara was happy they were talking again. Being angry with him had been incredibly distressing to her. She'd not wanted to fall out with him, but he had scared her so much! If she'd lost him…

Fastening the buckle, she stood up and tried to walk. But it was odd, because she still had a trainer on the other foot. So she sat back down and got rid of that, as well as the other sock, and put on the other pink shoe. She could barely walk. She wobbled a bit, and had to put her hand out to grab the rack and steady herself.

'Whoa! You okay?' Tom asked, smiling.

'It's like learning to walk again.'

'How do they feel?'

'Awful.'

'I'm not sure that colour would go with the dress.'

'Maybe they have them in gold? I could ask.'

'I think you should try a different heel. You don't look right in those.'

Oh. He didn't think she looked good. And nor did she feel good in them. Not really. They were uncomfortable, and they pinched, and the heel was doing something strenuous to her calf muscles.

Cara sat down to take them off.

'Try on the gold pair,' Tom said. 'What have you got to lose?'

'My ability to walk?'

She grabbed the high-heeled golden pair with reluctance, even though she could see they were beautiful shoes. Elegant…stylish… She just wished they weren't so high!

She tried standing and wobbled.

Tom took hold of her arm briefly, then let go.

Cara stood there, trying to keep her balance, but her centre of gravity seemed way off, all of a sudden, and she was afraid to move.

'They look great.'

'Of course you're going to say that. You're a man.'

'You don't think they look great?'

'I do. It's just… I'm not sure I can move. They're perfect if you plan on carrying me into the ball and then plonking me down by the bar, so I don't have to move all night.'

She blushed at the thought of him carrying her over his shoulder, fireman-style. Caveman-style? As if he'd chosen his woman and now she was his.

'Just try and move,' he said.

'Okay…'

Cara looked about her. No one was watching, so she wasn't about to make a colossal ass of herself. They were all too busy shopping for their own shoes, lost in their own little worlds. It was just her and Tom, and he stood in front of her like a proud parent, waiting for his toddler to take its first steps.

She took an awkward step, but it felt as if

she might snap the heel. She was so used to putting her heel down first, then her toe, but that just wasn't going to work. Not for her. Maybe she needed to somehow put the heel and toe down together?

She took another awkward step, and then another, but then her ankle wobbled, and her balance went, and she was suddenly falling forward into Tom's arms.

He caught her, saving her from faceplanting down on the floor. But now she found herself in another strange predicament.

She was in his arms, her head against his chest, hearing his heart pound inside his ribcage. And it was beating fast. Probably from the shock of her falling, that was all. She could feel the muscles in his body...could smell his body spray—something masculine and earthy that performed wonders on her senses. Her cheeks flushed and she looked up into his eyes. Something strange passed through them, and she was so caught in his magnetism she forgot to pull away. Forgot to try and move. Forgot to try and operate her feet.

Because being in his arms like this...so close she could feel every breath...it was a heady place to be.

'Thanks, I...'

His lips were parted and his eyes were large as he stared down at her, but eventually common sense kicked in. He didn't feel anything for her! That was nonsense! He'd just caught her because she'd tripped—that was all!

She coloured and pushed away from him, let go. And somehow, awkwardly, she made her way back to her seat, bending over to slowly undo the buckles, so that her hair would hide her face, her blushing cheeks, the pounding of her own heart.

I wanted to kiss him.

Had he been able to see that? Had she given her feelings away?

She'd wanted it so much. How romantic would that have been? But romance never found Cara. It never had—why would now be any different? Especially with someone who was so off-limits? Her best friend.

Victoria would have been able to handle these heels. She'd have glided down a red carpet. She'd have made her father proud. Tom must think that she was an absolute idiot. Trying to be something that she was not.

'Ankles okay?' he asked, his voice sounding deep and breathy.

'Yeah. They're…they're good, thanks.' She sat up, not sure where to look. She picked up the strappy gold sandals and placed them back on the shelf. 'Maybe we should keep looking?'

He nodded. 'Yeah. I'm parched. Are you parched? Should I fetch us a coffee?'

And he got up and left the shop.

Odd… But maybe he'd seen something in her gaze when he'd caught her, and now he felt awkward because he was going to have to say something about it? Tell her that he'd seen that look in her eyes and it could never happen? They were just friends?

Because it would be so embarrassing if he did. She'd have to protest and lie to him. Say, *Don't be silly! I just fell. Nothing happened… let's move on.*

There was no way she wanted to have *that chat* with him. But clearly he'd felt something, because he'd looked incredibly uncomfortable just now. Probably trying to work out just how he'd tell his friend that he didn't think of her in that way.

Oh, God. This is mortifying.

Tom stood waiting in the queue by the coffee cart, trying to calm his racing heart. Something weird had just happened with Cara. She'd tripped, and he'd caught her…but when he'd held her in his arms she'd looked up into his eyes and...

He swallowed hard. Had he been wrong? He'd thought he'd seen something written across her face—but he had to be imagining things, right? Because this was Cara! She didn't have any romantic feelings for him. And yet he could have sworn that he'd seen something in her eyes. Seen want. Seen desire. Seen...feelings.

But we're just friends.

Those were the parameters of their relationship and that was why they worked together so well. They both knew where they stood, and there was nothing romantic between them—there couldn't be. Maybe he was just being sensitive because they'd had that falling out earlier and emotions had been running high.

He'd reached the front of the queue. 'Two lattes, please.'

Should he say something when he got back to the shoe shop? Should he just pretend that nothing had happened? That seemed cowardly, but he really didn't want to run the risk of making their relationship awkward. He'd hate that. He needed to be able to see her. Needed to have her in his life. If he ruined it he'd never forgive himself.

He headed back to the shop, determined to act as if nothing untoward had ever happened between them.

Cara knew she couldn't risk anything like that happening again, and she kind of wanted the evening to be over—so she could get home and take a bath, or something, pretend that everything was normal. So what if the shoes were too high? All she needed was practice walking in them, and she could do that at home. There was still a week or two before the ball.

So she took the high-heeled shoes to the till to pay for them, and rummaged for her phone when it began to ring.

She had a sudden fear that the caller might be Tom. That he'd gone home, too embarrassed to face her. But when she pulled the phone from her pocket she saw that it was her father.

Great. Just what I need right now.

'Hello?'

'Cara, darling! How are you? Have I caught you at a good time?'

'Sure. I'm just out shoe-shopping.'

'For the ball? Marvellous. I'm so looking forward to it. Seeing you there with all your brothers. The whole family back together again.'

'Is there anything in particular I can help you with?' She didn't mean to sound so sharp with him.

'No, no… I just thought I'd let you know about the latest arrangements. I've been speaking with Hodge, your boss. I know he suggested a deejay or something for the evening, but due to the ball being at the manor I thought a deejay might be a bit tacky, so I've organised an orchestra to come instead.'

She blinked. An *orchestra*? 'Dad…'

'Oh, it was no bother. Nothing fancy—just a local group. But I thought I'd let you know so that you could practise your dancing.'

'Dancing?' She looked down at the heels in her hands. She could barely *walk*.

'You know…waltzes and things. Your mother loved all of that—it will be a fitting tribute. Plus, it will be lovely for people to get on the dance floor and enjoy themselves… not feel like they're only there to open their wallets.'

'Right. Dancing.'

She looked up. She could see Tom coming her way, holding two coffee cups. Dancing. In that dress. With those heels? She'd be

clutching onto Tom all night! A few seconds
had been awkward enough. How would she
ever hide how she felt all night?

Was it too late to get out of going alto-
gether?

The fire engine raced through the dark streets,
lighting up houses in flashes of red and blue.
They were heading to an industrial estate
behind the one where that guy had caught
his arm in the printing press. Ahead of them
they could see the night sky lit up by orange
flames, with plumes of thick black smoke billowing upwards.

Cara hoped it wasn't the paper factory,
because if it was then the fire was going to
be intense, with all that flammable material
around it, fuelling the flames.

Originally, she hadn't been meant to work
this night shift, but she'd offered to work
overtime as one of Blue Watch was off sick
and Cara didn't feel she wanted to be sitting
at home worrying about Tom and the upcom-
ing ball. The whole situation was driving her
crazy, and she'd had a headache all day. Every
time she thought she'd got on top of her racing
thoughts and sorted out how she was meant
to be feeling, another thing came along and
shook the ground beneath her feet.

When Tom had got back to the shoe shop with the coffees he'd seemed surprised that she was buying the gold shoes that she'd just fallen over in, but he'd said okay when she'd told him that practice would make perfect, and then she'd said she was tired and could they go home?

They'd driven home in silence—a comfortable silence that time—but still her heart had been racing and she hadn't told him about the dancing. He'd barely been able to hold her for a few seconds without looking alarmed. If he heard that her father was meddling again and now wanted them to learn how to dance... Well, she didn't want to see Tom trying to get out of their fake date. It would be embarrassing. Better to just turn up on the night and act surprised, suffer through one dance with him and then go home.

She'd have done her duty to her father and her mother and to the Websters, whose night it actually was going to be. They deserved help to find the best home they could afford. She would do it for them. And if she ended up with a twisted ankle at the end of the night because of it...? Well, fine.

As the appliance pulled up at the fire, another two fire engines that had been called from neighbouring stations arrived, and Hodge leapt out to co-ordinate with the other chief fire officers as Cara and the others began to prepare the hoses.

Hodge came back and gave them their instructions. 'Okay, I want you two over here, taking the east corner of the building. Garrett? They're a man down on Red Watch—can you help them on the west corner?'

Garrett ran over to help the others.

Cara felt the surge of the water as it ran through the pipe and aimed it at the flames, feeling the heat from the fire as it roared high into the sky. The ceiling of the industrial unit already had holes in where the flames had burnt through.

Hodge was yelling. 'Looks like we have a missing night guard! Cara? You're with me. We're going to head round the back and start our search at the guard box.'

Cara passed the hose to Reed and set off at a run with Hodge. They had to give the building a wide berth, mindful of the danger of collapse, and when they got to the guard box it was empty. A half-drunk cup of coffee was cooling on the table inside.

'Damn. Where is he?' Hodge grabbed a timesheet off the wall. 'Looks like he makes laps of the building at midnight, three and five a.m.'

She checked her watch. A quarter past midnight. 'Think he's inside?' she asked.

They both looked to the building, almost consumed in flames.

'I sincerely hope not,' said Hodge.

By the time they got back to the front of the building, several ambulances and Tom in his rapid response car had arrived.

Her stomach turned at the thought of facing him again, so she went to help with the hoses. The water was having some effect, and they were able to move forward to beat back some of the flames.

As she watched, one of Red Watch came out of the building, carrying someone over his shoulder. The missing night guard? She hoped so. As she moved forward a few more steps she glanced over briefly. Saw Tom ministering to the unconscious patient, placing an oxygen mask over his nose.

I can't concentrate on Tom. I need to focus on what I'm doing.

It felt like a sucker punch to the gut when Tom saw Cara look his way and then turn without acknowledging him at all. He tried to tell himself it was because she was concentrating on her job. Not to read anything into it. But things had been strange between them ever since her fall in the shoe shop.

And that niggled—because he'd spent the entire night tossing and turning in his bed, telling himself that he'd somehow made up the whole thing. But if she *was* avoiding him… Maybe she was embarrassed. Had she seen the look in his eyes when he'd caught her? Maybe she was *appalled*?

There's a fire that needs putting out. She's not going to stop and come over and talk to me.

But a smile might have been nice. A nod of the head.

Something was up. He could feel it.

He turned his mind to his patient. He had some mild burns to his hands, and his respirations were extremely low due to smoke inhalation. He had soot in his throat and up his nostrils. God only knew what sort of chemicals he might have breathed in through the smoke. It all depended upon what was burning.

He helped get the man onto a trolley and whisked off into an ambulance, which roared away from him to get him to an Accident and Emergency department.

He hoped the man would live. It seemed

they'd got to him in time. But life could be a fragile thing. Tom knew the truth of that better than most.

The fire was extinguished. Only smoke continued to fill the sky. Cara finally had a moment to shuck off her helmet, unzip her coat and allow some of the cool night air to flow in around her body.

She loved her job. She loved to battle against the flames. And although this fire had taken a few hours it was all under control now. The fire investigation team would soon arrive, but Hodge had already come out and said it looked as if some kind of accelerant had deliberately been spilled in the warehouse. He'd found the flashpoint of the fire and the night guard had been found near that.

Whether the guard had started the fire, or someone else had, she didn't know, but the report from the hospital had already told them that the guard was alive but refusing to talk to the police. So…

'Hey.'

She turned. It was Tom. Her heart instantly began to thud again.

'Hey.' She looked away from him awkwardly, back at the blackened building that was now mostly in disarray.

'That was a tough one,' he said.

'It was.'

'I'm exhausted. Looking forward to going home and getting a shower.'

She nodded. A shower sounded great. A shower with Tom would be even better. But that wasn't going to happen anytime soon, so she said nothing about it.

'Gage away?'

'At my parents.' They're going on a cruise tomorrow and taking him with them. They'll be gone for three days.'

'You'll miss him.'

He nodded.

'So will I.'

Another nod.

'Are we okay?' Tom asked.

Her heart leapt into her throat, then began to thump against her ribs. 'Yeah! Of course we are!'

'Good. It's just things have seemed a little funny after…' He tailed off.

'I tripped. That's all. I've just got some other stuff on my mind.'

'Anything I can help with?'

She smiled. Despite it all, he was still willing to help her out. And she couldn't hold it in any longer. 'My father wants me to practise my waltz. He's organised an orchestra for the ball.'

'You know how to dance?'

She laughed. 'Oh, of course! I can cha-cha-cha with the best of them!'

'Really?'

Cara groaned. 'No. I have two left feet. Two left feet that are going to be in vertiginous heels. What do you think?'

Tom seemed to think for a moment. 'That I'm going to need steel-capped shoes.'

'And then some.'

She paused. She wanted to give him an out. Rather than hear him try to worm his way out of his obligation, it would be kinder to just let the man off the hook herself.

'You don't have to do this, you know... I can go alone. You can dance with someone who won't break every bone in your feet, and I will weather the storm with Xander, or Peregrine, or whoever my father tries to set me up with.'

'Are you kidding? I gave you my word. And I don't back out of any promises I make.'

'You sure? I'm not sure our relationship will survive my trying to dance with you.'

She couldn't tell him the real reason. That she wasn't sure *she'd* survive being in his arms all night and not being able to kiss him, or touch him the way that she'd want to, or whisper sweet nothings into his ear.

Tom thought for a moment, then smiled. 'I have an idea.'

'Ditch the night entirely? I can't.' She grimaced.

'No, not that. Daphne—my sister-in-law. She can be our secret weapon.'

'And Daphne will be our secret weapon *how*, exactly?'

'She's a dance instructor. She owns Mango Dance Studio. She could teach you how to waltz.'

A dance instructor? Hmm...

'I know that place. It always looks busy. You think she'll have time to help me?'

'I can but ask.'

'Okay, but be realistic with her, okay? Don't tell her I have promise, or anything. Tell her she's getting a complete newbie, with no sense of rhythm or grace. Tell her I'm like a baby elephant. Or a hippo. Or some other animal that wouldn't be able to dance well but could break her partner's toes.'

He gave her a playful nudge. 'You're not a hippo. Or an elephant. A few hours with Daphne and you'll be as graceful as a swan.'

'You remember me in those heels, though, right?'

'I do.'

'I guess it's too late to find a stunt double?'

He laughed, and she loved the sound of it. Loved how they were talking normally again.

'Much too late. Besides…' He looked directly into her eyes, his voice softening, 'I'm looking forward to dancing with you.'

Her breath caught in her throat. 'You are?'

Did he mean that? And *how* did he mean that? As friends? Or…?

No, it can never be as something more. This man has danced with Victoria. I've seen the wedding video! They were perfect. Graceful.

'Are you kidding me? You'll be the belle of the ball.'

She liked it that he was trying to build up her confidence. He was a good man.

'And you'll stay by my side all night? Because I'm not sure I'll be able to stand upright after dancing in those heels.'

'Always.'

She smiled back at him, then looked away. Because looking into his eyes right now was making all those other thoughts come back. The thoughts she shouldn't be having about Tom. He truly was a gentleman. Her knight in shining armour. But he was also a grieving widower, and she was a very bad person for even entertaining these thoughts about him right now.

'You can dance,' she said. 'I've seen you.'

He shrugged. 'I think I've got some moves.'

Cara nodded. Yes, he had. But even if he hadn't he'd still be a better dancer than her. If the worst came to the worst, she'd throw off her heels and dance with him barefoot, if need be.

Anything to be in his arms a moment longer.

CHAPTER SEVEN

THE MANGO DANCE STUDIO was just off the high street, situated above a Turkish supermarket and a pawn shop.

Cara hadn't been sure what to wear for a practice dance session. The only dance movies she'd seen were set in the past, where leotards and leg warmers were all the rage, but she was pretty sure they weren't in the eighties any more, so she'd decided her usual gym gear would have to do. A sports bra under a baggy long-sleeved tee shirt and some tracksuit bottoms, with trainers.

In a bag, she carried the vertiginous golden heels, in case this Daphne told her that she needed to practise in those, but she really hoped that wasn't the case. Every time she put them on she could feel blisters wanting to make their appearance on her little toes, and her ankles ached in wary anticipation.

And she was also anxious about meeting Daphne. If she was Tom's sister-in-law, that meant she was Victoria's sister, and that meant Daphne would no doubt be curious about this woman Tom was bringing and what their relationship was. She didn't want Daphne to hate her, or to see something that Cara was desperately trying to hide.

As time ticked on she knew she couldn't leave it any longer, so Cara opened the door that had Mango Dance Studio blazoned across it and headed up a narrow set of stairs.

Once inside, she was amazed. The stairwell was painted in a light grey, and as she took the stairs she saw framed photo after framed photo of dancers in various shows. Ballet, tap…something from the West End, by the looks of it. An entire cast taking a bow in front of a standing ovation, and at the top of the stairs a few dancers standing with celebrities, the photos autographed.

Daphne was serious about her business, clearly. She had ambitions for her dancers, and this exhibition of photos let everyone know that.

At the top of the stairs was a glass door. Cara pulled it open and walked straight into a reception area, where a petite blonde sat behind a desk adorned with orchids.

'Can I help you?'

'I'm here to see Daphne. I have a private session with her.'

'Name?'

'Cara Maddox.'

'Oh, they're waiting for you! Go through the door on the right there and to the end of the corridor.'

Tom must have already arrived. She smiled her thanks to the receptionist and headed down the corridor. Again, there were pictures on the walls. Large poster-sized, this time. Dancers in a production of *Swan Lake*. A line of female dancers all on tippy-toes, arms gracefully arced overhead. Something Christmassy that she didn't know. And another that looked as if it was set in the nineteen-twenties. The costumes were amazing, and all the dancers looked happy and proud.

Could Daphne make Cara look that good?

But as she got closer to the studio door her nerves kicked in big-time, and she froze, her hand on the handle, ready to push the door open but worrying about who and what waited for her on the other side. Tom had a relationship with this woman. She was his sister-in-law. Would Daphne hate her? Think she was replacing her beloved Victoria?

She almost turned back. This whole event was crazy enough as it was! But, unwilling to let her father get any satisfaction from Cara failing them all yet again, she yanked the door open, lifted her chin and went in.

Tom was at the far end of the room, in a pair of dark tracksuit bottoms and a tee shirt, laughing with a tall, svelte, Amazonian woman who was the spitting image of Victoria.

Cara felt a jolt to her system, her mouth went dry, and she suddenly needed a drink very, very badly.

Daphne was the perfect embodiment of Victoria. Every reminder of why Tom had married his wife. She was tall and beautiful and slim. Perky and graceful and stylish. She wore a leotard top that moulded her perfect breasts and showed off her slim waist, attached to which was a diaphanous black skirt that just covered her bottom and hips. And below that were long, slim but strong legs.

'Cara! You made it!'

Tom came over to give her a hug and a quick peck on the cheek, but she was too nervous to enjoy it, her eyes clamped onto Daphne, who was watching the entire thing curiously. She was so keen to give the right impression Tom's kiss hardly registered.

'Wouldn't miss it. Hello, Daphne. I'm Cara!' she blurted, holding out her hand for

Daphne to shake. 'Are you sure you can teach this old dog some new tricks?'

Why was she being so self-deprecating? Was she trying to tell to Daphne that she was nothing special? That Victoria's memory would never be threatened by her?

Perhaps I ought to have completed the image by tripping over my own feet walking in?

'Of course. Cara. Tom's told me so much about you.'

'All good, I hope.' She couldn't stop smiling. She felt like one of those ventriloquist's dummies, her face etched with a permanent rictus grin.

'Tom never speaks badly about anybody.'

Good. That was good. And of course she was right. He didn't. She couldn't recall him badmouthing anyone.

'Great.' She glanced at Tom and could see he was looking at her with amusement.

'So, shall we get started?' Daphne asked.

'Let's do that,' Cara agreed.

'Have you ever danced before?'

Cara set the bag of heels down on the floor by the piano. 'No. Well, I had to do a show once at school, but I'm not sure that counts.'

'Do you ever dance when you're alone?'

'No. I'd rather go to the gym and lift some weights.'

'How much can you bench press?'

'About a hundred kilos.'

'Impressive! You're strong. Tom tells me you're a firefighter, so I guess you have to be?'

'Yes, but I enjoy it. It's not a chore for me, going to the gym.'

'Good. So you're not afraid of hard work?'

Cara shook her head. 'No.'

'Excellent. Because that is what's ahead of you. So! Let's get started. Tom says you need to know how to waltz, so before we can get into how to do box steps and fleckerls and spin turns we need to perfect the hold. Tom, would you join us?'

Box steps? Fleck-what? Perfect the hold?

That meant being up close and personal with Tom. In front of Daphne! What had she and Victoria been? Twins, or something? Surely she'd remember if Victoria had had a twin? She couldn't remember such a fact, but maybe she'd forgotten?

And right now it very much felt as if Victoria herself was standing there, asking Cara to get into 'hold' with Tom.

'For a standard waltz we need you in a closed frame hold, like this.'

Daphne began positioning them like man-nequins. Pushing her and Tom closer to-gether, linking their hands, adjusting elbows, straightening backs, shifting hips, until she felt they were perfect.

Cara couldn't recall ever being this close to Tom.

Daphne stood back, like a sculptor admir-ing her handiwork. 'Perfect. Now, you'll need to hold this frame throughout.'

Cara glanced at Tom and smiled nervously before looking away. She was up close and personal with Tom. Tom's right hand was under her left shoulder blade. Her left hand rested on top of Tom's shoulder blade. Their bodies were in contact, though they were both slightly off to the right of each other.

'Stop looking at one another. In this dance you both look off to the left,' Daphne said firmly.

Okay. That made it a bit easier. It would have been hard to have her body pressed against his and look at him, too. Thank God her father had told her she'd need to know a waltz, and not a tango or a rumba. She'd seen those on that television show, and there was no way she'd have been able to do either of those with Tom without becoming a gibber-ing mess.

'You neck looks broken, Cara. Tom doesn't want to look like he's dancing with a zombie. Do it like this.' Daphne tweaked her neck, elongating it. 'This is a dance of grace and softness. Imagine you're exposing your neck so that a man may plant a kiss there.'

Cara flushed, imagining Tom doing just that. Could he feel the heat radiating from her cheeks? She must have squeezed him with her fingers, because Tom squeezed back, as if to say, *You've got this...don't worry.*

'Right, so now I'm going to teach you the left closed change and the right closed change. These are your most basic steps, all right?'

What followed next was the most gruelling thirty-minute session, during which Cara felt less and less that she was learning to dance, but more that she was against an army drill instructor. Daphne was kind and encouraging to Tom, complimenting him on his form and technique, whereas to Cara it seemed she was less accepting. Everything Cara did was wrong, or out of time, and she kept losing the basic form of their hold.

When she did that Daphne would step forward, pull Cara out of hold and insert herself into Tom's arms and say, 'Like this!'

Cara was beginning to feel like a little girl being told off by a strict headmistress, and inside her rage was beginning to build. She was trying her best! She'd never danced before! Couldn't this Daphne give her a *little* credit?

Cara was sweaty, and tired, and her arms ached from holding them in the correct position. She was tired of counting *one-two-three, one-two-three*, and thinking about how to place her feet, and maintain hold, and look to her left whilst going right, and holding her neck. And Daphne scolding her all the time implied that Tom's last dance partner—Victoria—had been a much better student.

'Can we take a break?'

Cara broke hold and walked away to the piano, where there was some water, and poured herself a drink. She knocked back the entire glass in one go and stood there, hands on hips, breathing hard. She hadn't known what to expect from this session, but she'd expected more enjoyment than this! She was dancing with Tom! Spending time with him up close and personal. And it was being ruined by his harsh task mistress of a sister-in-law!

'You'll never improve if you keep taking breaks,' admonished Daphne, smiling a perfect, un-sweaty smile.

'Yeah? Well, I'll never learn anything the way *you're* teaching me.'

Daphne looked to Tom, as if she couldn't quite believe the impudence. 'I'm sorry?'

'I'm not trying to be a professional dancer! I appreciate your time, Daphne, but you're teaching me like you're trying to get me into a top dance school or a show in the West End! It's just a ball at my father's home. It's meant to be fun!'

'You're not having fun?'

'No! I just want to learn the basics of the waltz, so that I don't fall over my feet in front of my family and friends. No one's going to be scoring me, and no one's going to kick me out of a competition if I accidentally step on Tom's toes! I just want...'

They were both staring at her.

'What?' asked Daphne.

'I want to dance with Tom and I want it to be fun.'

Cara looked to Tom and he gazed back at her with a smile, as if he was proud of her, and in that moment that was all that mattered. When Cara glanced at Daphne, her face said something different.

'I don't need you constantly shoving in my face the fact that Victoria could pick up dance steps easily. I don't need you telling me that I'm not as good as her. I'm not trying to replace Victoria!'

'I'm sorry. I'm not used to teaching for anything but competitions and getting people ready for auditions. Maybe I have been a little…harsh?'

Cara shook her head, wiping the sweat from her forehead with her forearm. 'I need the loo. Excuse me.' And she headed off to find a toilet, feeling humiliated and ashamed.

Had Daphne deliberately been trying to make Cara feel she wasn't good enough? Comparing her to her sister to show her that she could never have Tom, if that was her plan?

She hoped that in her absence Tom would stick up for her and fight her side.

Tom watched Cara go, and when the door closed he turned around and faced Daphne. 'She's right. You were being harsh.'

Daphne had the decency to look shame-faced. 'I'm sorry. It's just…when you said you were bringing this woman I felt like you were leaving my sister behind.'

'I will never forget my wife, Daphne. Never. But life moves on. I've moved on. And Cara is my best friend. She was there for me when no one else could be. She got me through those dark months and she still does it today.'

'You like her?'

'Of course I do! She's my best friend.' He stared at his sister-in-law, hoping that his other thoughts about Cara wouldn't give him away, but he wasn't sure he was that good an actor.

Dancing with Cara had been nerve-racking. A delight. Excitement overdrive. His pulse had been thrumming in the hundreds, without a doubt, and he'd kept sneaking glances at her, even though he'd been meant to look left, away from her. And some of those stumbles had been his fault, not hers.

'I kind of got the feeling she was more than a best friend and that scared me,' said Daphne.

'She's not,' he said, feeling his cheeks flush with the lie.

'Well, if there is ever a chance that you could be something more with this girl, then... you should take it. I want you to be happy, Tom. Victoria would want you and Gage to be happy, too.'

Tom stared at her. He was glad of her kind words, but still all he could feel was doubt. Doubt that he should be moving on already... doubt that he should put his friendship with Cara at risk. What if they did try going out with each other and it all fell apart because he wasn't good enough for her? He'd failed at being with Victoria. Who was to say being with Cara would be any better? He'd been a bad partner.

And why was he even thinking about any of this when he had no idea how Cara felt anyway? She might laugh in his face at the suggestion that they be more than friends, and he wasn't sure he could stand the rejection. And, maybe it was cowardly of him, but he liked how they were right now. He liked seeing her most days, being able to talk to her and share his life with her. And all those secret feelings…? Well, they felt good, too. He could carry on like this even if it did torture him day after day.

Cara was great. Not only with him, but with his son, too. Gage loved Cara. Adored her. She would fit into his little family easily if she was given the opportunity.

Listen to me! I haven't even asked her out and I'm already imagining us as a family!

But that was a good thing, right? That he could visualise it?

'Thanks. I appreciate it,' he said now.

'She's different,' said Daphne.

'Yes, she is.' He smiled, thinking of how different Cara was. Cara was…unique. And quirky. Not your typical girly girl. But he loved that. Loved her strength. Loved the fact that she had no idea how beautiful she actually was. Her innocence on that matter was engaging.

'And maybe different is what you need?' Daphne suggested. 'I know you and Vic had your problems.'

But what someone needed and what they wanted were two different things. Did he have all these feelings for Cara because he needed her? Was he using her to make himself feel good about the fact that he could help her when he hadn't been able to help his own wife?

Normally when he was having doubts about something he would talk to Cara and get her opinion, but on this he couldn't.

Why do I have such trouble telling the women who are important to me how I really feel?

Cara had splashed her face with water and was now standing in the studio bathroom, staring at her reflection in the mirror and wishing she'd never had that outburst with Daphne. She'd been trying to help, teaching in the only way she knew how. It wasn't her fault that Cara couldn't dance and was having difficulty picking up form and rhythm.

I'll go back in there and apologise.

She patted her face with a paper towel, gave herself one last stern look in the mirror and readied herself for delivering a heartfelt apology. She'd not only embarrassed herself, she'd also put Tom in an awkward position with his sister-in-law. Cara had never meant to cause trouble. That wasn't who she was.

When she reopened the door to the studio music was playing. She recognised the music and could even—miracle upon miracle— count the three-beat, as if her brain had somehow been switched on after Daphne's instruction.

Tom and Daphne were dancing the waltz in the middle of the room and she stood watching them, a smile on her face, wishing she could be as graceful.

When they saw her they broke apart and Tom walked over to her with a smile. 'You okay?'

'I'm fine. And I'm sorry. I didn't mean to raise my voice back there.'

'Don't worry about it. Daphne has something she wants to say.'

'Oh?' She turned to Daphne, who was walking towards her like a dancer, all long-limbed and flowy. Graceful, like a swan. It was in her bearing and her stature, after years upon years of knowing how to make her body move in an attractive way.

'Cara. I want to apologise one last time.'

'Oh, there's no need for you to—'

'There's every need. I was unnecessarily harsh towards you and that was wrong. I want to help you and Tom learn to dance so that it's fun.' She smiled. 'Take Tom's hand.'

Cara couldn't believe it! Flushing, she stepped into hold with Tom, feeling the strength and kindness of his grip, the press of his firm body against hers, seeing the reassuring look he gave her. Her back protested a little. Her neck ached and her arms felt heavy from all the practice.

But Daphne stepped back and said, 'Listen to the music. Just go with the flow. See what happens.'

So they began to dance.

It was awkward to begin with. Cara stepped on Tom's toes twice. Grimacing, apologising, her cheeks going red every time. But Daphne and Tom both encouraged her to continue, and eventually she began to get the basic box step.

'We're doing it!' she said. 'We're actually bloody doing it!'

Daphne clapped, then strode over to the

piano when a trill came from her bag. Cara and Tom stopped dancing.

Daphne looked at her phone. 'Ah, sorry, guys. I've got to go. My husband is not so politely reminding me we have tickets to see a show tonight.'

'Oh!' Cara went to get her own bag, with the heels in it. 'We'll let you lock up, then.'

'No, no! Both of you continue! Naomi doesn't lock up the studio until eight. You've plenty of time to practice.'

'Oh, well… If you're sure?'

'Absolutely! It's been a pleasure to meet you, Cara.'

And Daphne kissed her on both cheeks and rushed from the studio, her diaphanous skirt billowing behind her.

Alone with Tom in the studio, Cara turned to look at him and laughed nervously. 'You want to continue?'

'I don't see why not.'

'All right…'

She nervously stepped forward to take Tom's hand and get into hold. Now they were alone together it all seemed so different from when they'd had a chaperone in Daphne. It felt more intimate, his hand in hers… More personal, her body against his.

Forbidden.

Her heart pounded in her chest—so much so, she was convinced he'd be able to feel it, reverberating through his ribcage, and she didn't dare look at him. It was easier to pretend that he wasn't there, to look off to the left and try to remember her steps.

The music continued to play. They stepped forward, right, together. Left, forward, together. She muffled an apology for stepping on his toes once again, but then they began to get the hang of it. Cara was beginning to remember the flow, now, and feeling more comfortable, more able. And when Tom began to make a turn, going in a different direction, she followed easily, happy to be led.

The music was bright and happy, and it made her think of sunshine, and fields full of wildflowers, dancing in a soft breeze. She and Tom were the wildflowers. She became comfortable in his hold, laughed when they turned, began to feel the joy of being at one in partnership with him.

If only life could stay like this for ever.

They began to find an easy sway, moving with the music as it built. They were both smiling and laughing at how easy they were finding it in each other's arms.

'We're doing it!' she said.

'We certainly are.'

'Think we should try it with me in the heels?'

She didn't want to break contact with him. She didn't want to stop at all. But dancing in trainers must be easier than it would be in the heels, and although she felt she'd got a good grip on the dance so far, it needed to be rooted in reality.

'Let's give it a go.'

They broke apart, Cara feeling breathless, but full of excitement and drive. She quickly put on the heels, grimacing at the way they made her feet feel. She'd been practising wearing them. Wanted to show Tom she could walk in them now—even if they did make her feel as if she was about to have the worst blisters in the world.

'Wow! Look at you!'

She liked the way he looked her up and down. He was looking at her as if she was a woman, not just his best friend. She saw appreciation in his eyes. Saw...*want*? That made her heart palpitate!

Cara stepped forward and into his arms once again. Her centre of gravity was off, but it didn't take her long to adjust. In Tom's arms, she felt she could do anything. Be any-one. Even a graceful dancer. They swayed and danced, bodies pressed close, enjoying the rhythm of the music, enjoying the feel of being in each other's arms. And as the music came to a crescendo Tom twirled her round and pulled her close, smiling at her, and the intensity of his eyes, so close to her own, caused her heart to pitter-patter.

They stood staring at each other, mere inches apart, but their bodies pressed close. She couldn't help herself. She looked down at his lips. They were parted. He was breathless. And the way he was looking back at her… as if he wanted her… It did strange things to her insides. She reached up, stroked the side of his face, trailed her fingers over his square jaw, and suddenly, somehow, they were kiss-ing.

Her mind was going crazy at what was happening. Disbelief. Surprise. Awe. Terror. Kissing Tom was everything she'd imagined it would be. His lips were soft, his kiss passion-ate, as if he'd been keeping a secret desire for her hidden and it was now being unleashed, and he was taking every moment of the kiss to enjoy it, in case it ended too soon.

She knew how he felt. She didn't want it to end, either.

Her fingers went into his hair, and he growled deep in his throat, and the sound just turned her on even more. The rest of the world disappeared with the intensity of their kiss. All that existed, all that mattered, was the fact that they were together and that somehow this magical moment was happening. She didn't stop to think of the consequences. She didn't stop to think of what would happen *after* the kiss. All she could think of was his lips on hers, his tongue in her mouth and the way he felt in her arms.

That was enough.

That was all she needed and would ever need in that singular moment.

And then…they both came up for air.

Breathing heavily, Cara stared into Tom's eyes, seeing the want and the need. The real world came crashing back in. The dance studio. Who they were and what they were doing. How they had just changed things between them for evermore.

'What does this mean?' Tom asked, gazing back into her eyes, his hands sitting on her waist.

'I think it means…that maybe we are something more than friends.'

Tom looked down at the ground. 'Is that possible?'

Cara gave a hesitant smile. 'Let's find out.'

It was the day of Gage's birthday party. His grandparents had just brought him back from their three-day cruise to Bruges, and he had returned with a dazzling array of different types of chocolate that he'd bought from the chocolate shops in the Belgian city.

Tom was so glad to have him back. He'd missed him incredibly. Without Gage at home, it had been as if he was living a different life lately. That of a single guy. He'd gone out dancing. Kissed a girl. And now he thought that he might be in a relationship of some kind. His life had gone off in a direction he wasn't sure of.

After he'd kissed Cara, the receptionist had opened the door to the studio and reminded them that she'd be closing up soon. So they'd both very quickly separated and nodded and begun packing up. He'd kept looking at Cara, his heart pounding, his head spinning with possibilities. He'd wanted to say more, to ask her questions, but he'd known it couldn't be a late night—and did he really want to send this blossoming *something* into a downward spiral so soon?

He didn't think they'd ended it awkwardly, but his head was full of questions. What did this mean? Had they stepped over a line that neither of them should have crossed? Could they ever go back to just being friends if this went south somehow?

He didn't want to think it would go bad, but he had no other point of reference. He'd only ever been in a relationship with Victoria and he'd lost her. Their romance had soured soon after the rings had gone on each other's fingers. But that was just life, right? It couldn't be sunshine and roses every day.

Or could it? Maybe it was possible—if you found the right person? His grandparents had never had a cross word between them, and they'd held hands right up until the end of their days. When his nan had left this world his grandfather had pined so much he'd died of a broken heart just weeks later.

That was the kind of love Tom wanted.

But right now he was in his worst nightmare. A soft play centre. He'd tried to steer Gage away from the idea, but when he had asked his son where he wanted the party Gage had said here, so... He was willing to grit his teeth and get through it.

Gage had invited his entire class from preschool, so there were about twenty-five children. He'd had to sit and make up party bags for them all, and most seemed to have arrived. The play centre was filled with noise and that odd smell of sweat and plastic as children whizzed down slides or swung Tarzan-style into a deep ball pit.

Gage himself had just come down a slide. 'Did you see me, Daddy?'

'I did.'

'I did it head-first!'

He smiled. 'I saw.'

And then he sensed more than saw Cara's arrival. As if his body was attuned, he felt her coming through the swing doors, holding a brightly wrapped parcel that she passed to him.

'Hey.'

'Hey, yourself.'

'Cara!' Gage barrelled into her arms and Cara swung him up and around easily, making him laugh.

'Hey, squirt!'

'You came!'

Cara put him down on the ground. 'You bet I did! I wouldn't miss this, would I?'

'Are you coming in? I want to show you my secret hidey spot!'

She nodded. Glanced at Tom. 'Lead the way.'

Gage ran off into the netted maze, bounding up some soft rubber steps before turning to see that she was following. 'You coming?'

'Yep!' Cara turned and looked shyly at Tom. 'You okay?'

'More than okay.'

He smiled. Things were still good with them. She didn't seem to have had any second thoughts. No one had put any doubts into her head. He was both glad and scared. It meant that they were going to go somewhere with this thing they were building between them.

'I'd better go.'

He nodded. 'Yes, you should.'

He watched her scramble away after his son, loving how Gage took her hand and began to drag her deeper into the maze until he lost sight of them both.

Could he ask for anything more right now?

They were both good. Neither had regrets. And his son *adored* Cara.

So why did he feel as if he was standing on the edge of an abyss?

Cara offered to carry an exhausted Gage up to bed.

'Oh, you don't need to do that,' Tom protested.

'It's my pleasure. I haven't read to him in ages.'

She'd missed the little squirt, knowing he was away for a few days, and that she couldn't see him. But it had been nice too. It had enabled her and Tom to get close. That kiss had been... Well... She kept replaying it in her head. Over and over.

Tom had kissed her back!

She hadn't imagined that part. She hadn't dreamed it. It had been *real*, and he'd seemed to want her as much as she had been wanting him. Which was crazy and wild and...

Part of her had worried that when she turned up for Gage's party Tom might be awkward with her, might have had second thoughts, and would take her to one side and tell her that the kiss could never happen again. Only he hadn't.

She'd played with Gage for a bit, then stood with the parents. And when no one had been watching she'd brushed the side of her hand up against Tom's. It had been exciting, feeling that secret contact, knowing that no one else knew what was going on. It had been their own private thing. And when the children had all sat down to eat their chicken nuggets, or their burger and chips, Tom had squeezed past her in the party room, and the feel of his hand brushing over her hip had been electrifying.

In the car on their way home Gage had babbled away non-stop about what a great party it had been, and how much he had enjoyed his birthday, and Cara had felt glad. He'd not been a sad little boy who missed his mum. He'd been happy and bright and he'd enjoyed himself, and that had been a delight for her, too.

As she laid Gage down in his bed he yawned, and grabbed his teddy bear for a snuggle. Cara sat beside him and began to read him a story. It was often the highlight of her day, reading to Gage at night. She'd not realised how much she enjoyed it until he'd gone away and she hadn't been able to do it. Not realised how often she actually did it.

It didn't take too long for the little boy's eyes to grow heavy, and when his breathing became steady and his eyelids flickered with delightful dreams she crept off his bed, laid the book down on his bedside table and silently left his room, pulling the door almost shut, so that a sliver of light from the hall would show in his room.

When she turned round, Tom was waiting for her, smiling, and he reached up to tuck some of her hair behind her ear.

'He's had a great birthday, thanks to you.'

'It wasn't anything to do with me. You organised everything. I just showed up.'

'Showed up and managed to chase him around that massive jungle gym for almost two hours. Honestly, I don't know where you find the energy.'

'There's always energy if it's something you enjoy.'

She was finding it difficult to concentrate right now. Tom kept touching her. Her hair, her ear, her neck... Now his hand dropped to her waist and pulled her closer, and she almost stopped breathing. How often had she dreamed of this? Wanted this? What was going to happen?

Because if he was going to kiss her again, then maybe they should take this downstairs. Kissing, she could cope with. Kissing Tom had been wonderful the last time, and her lips burned to feel his upon hers again. But if it was going to be something else...

Cara hadn't been with anyone since Leo, and Leo had said some pretty hurtful things about her physical appearance. Things she knew she ought not to let affect her, but they did. Of course they did. How could they not? Tom might like kissing her, and dancing with her, but if he saw her naked would *he* think she looked too masculine, too?

She had short arms, short, stocky legs, almost no boobs to speak of, and muscles

aplenty. Her body was solid. Not much wobbled or was soft. Leo had said to her that no
straight man would want to be with a woman
who looked like a guy. That she wasn't as
feminine as she should be. That she wasn't
as graceful. And Tom had been with Victoria
his entire life, and she had been an elegant,
tall Amazon. Blonde and sylph-like. If she'd
had pointed ears she might have been an elf.
Beautiful. Ethereal. Cara had muscles and
tattoos and abs...

What if I'm not woman enough for him?

Tom reached out and pulled Gage's door
closed properly.

'What are you doing?'

'I don't want him to hear us.'

'Hear us doing what?'

Tom smiled and pulled her closer, his lips
nuzzling her neck, sending delicious shivers
down her body.

She closed her eyes in bliss, wanting to
give herself up to it, wanting to feel she could
be confident in her own body. But she'd always let people down in that way. Her mum
had wanted her to be more of a girl, to dress
in pink and enjoy the things she did, and she'd
gone against that. Playing with her brothers,
going hunting, making dens and playing sol-
diers. Most of her friends were guys and now

she was a firefighter, pumping iron in the gym, happy in jeans and trainers or combat boots rather than being the lady her mother had wanted. Leo had said she'd looked like more of a man than he did.

I can't compare to Victoria. I can't!

And so, although it pained her, although it ripped her in two, she pressed her hands against his chest and pushed him away.

'No. Stop. I'm sorry. I can't.'

'What is it?'

'I just... I can't.'

She turned from him and began to run down the stairs, heading for the front door.

CHAPTER EIGHT

Tom lay in bed alone, staring at the ceiling, wondering just what the hell had happened? They'd had such a great time at Gage's party. There'd been fun, and laughter, and Cara had been there, looking after his son as if it was her favourite job in the world, happily chasing him around the soft play area, joining in his games, never getting tired.

It had warmed his heart, the way the two of them got on, and it had left him free to socialise with the other parents—chat to them, share stories, and basically talk to other adults for an hour or two. About normal adult things.

He'd noticed the way one of the single mums looked at him. And that was nice, and all, but he'd only had eyes for one woman at the party. And there'd been moments when his arm had brushed Cara's, or their fingers had entwined, just briefly, and they'd shared a secret smile, when he'd felt whatever they had *building*. That build-up—the excitement, the anticipation of waiting to be alone with her—had been intoxicating.

They'd driven home, Cara had carried Gage up the stairs and read him a story, and he'd stood outside his son's bedroom door, listening to Cara doing all the voices for the characters and Gage's little chuckles. Cara made Gage happy. And she made *him* happy, too. He couldn't believe he'd fought this for so long, when clearly there was an attraction between them both. It had been exposed now, through that electrifying kiss, and he wanted more.

When Cara had crept from his son's bedroom, a smile upon her face, he'd just known he had to have her. The idea of spending some quality time in his own bedroom with her, slowly exploring her body and discovering what brought her pleasure, had given him so much excitement he'd thought he wouldn't be able to stand it.

That was why he'd had to touch her. Why he'd had to have contact. And he'd thought that she was enjoying it too. As he'd kissed her neck she had let out a little purr…or had it been a growl of pleasure? He'd exposed her neck even more, so that he could kiss her and taste her and imagine all the wonderfully naughty things he could do to her, and then…

Something had suddenly changed. She'd stiffened. Frozen. Placed her hands upon his chest and pushed him gently away. She'd looked…terrified!

'No. Stop. I'm sorry. I can't.'

Six words that had puzzled him, before she'd stepped past him, hurried down the stairs and disappeared out through the front door!

He'd gone after her. Of course he had.

'Cara!' he'd called.

How was she going to get home?

He'd texted her.

Come back. Please. Let's talk.

But there'd been no answer. No response. So all night he'd lain there, wondering what he'd done wrong. If he'd said something wrong. Or whether she'd simply got cold feet and maybe they were moving too fast.

That had to be it, right? All this time they'd been friends, and then they'd shared one kiss and suddenly he'd been doing things to her that he'd hoped would lead to sex. Perhaps she'd felt that too? Perhaps she'd panicked? Perhaps she feared taking that next step with him—because if they slept together and it wasn't great then there'd be no going back to their friendship.

He couldn't imagine that sex with Cara would be disappointing. His desire for her was almost overwhelming. Sometimes he felt he couldn't breathe. He wanted her so badly.

Or maybe it's that bastard Leo's fault? Those things he said to her. The way he made her feel about herself afterwards. Like she isn't woman enough.

Tom had done his best to build her up, build her confidence and self-esteem, but perhaps she still felt scared? He could only reassure her so much, Cara had to take that final step herself, and believe that she was woman enough for anyone.

Tom hoped that she'd had a good night's sleep and that maybe, just maybe, he'd get the chance to see her today and talk things over. Make her feel a little easier about things. Let her dictate the pace.

Feeling more optimistic, he managed an hour's sleep before his alarm woke him up for work.

Cara kept stirring her tea. Standing in the small kitchen of the fire station, she stared at the hot drink, her mind a thousand miles away.

'Earth to Cara?'

Reed's voice finally cut into her reverie. 'What?'

He laughed. 'You've been stirring that drink for about four minutes now. Something you want to talk about?'

There was. But not to him. Never to a man like him. She trusted Reed, in that he was her colleague and a damned fine firefighter. She would happily place her life in his hands and know that he had her back in such a situation. But as a friend? A *confidante*? No chance.

She put down the spoon and picked up the mug, carrying it over to the table. 'Not really. Not to you, anyway.'

He mimed being stabbed in the chest. 'Oof! That hurts.'

She smiled and sipped at her drink.

'Problems with *Daddy*?'

Cara ignored him.

'Too many Lords chasing after our fair Lady?'

'Shut up, Reed.'

'Or is it lover-boy causing all your problems?'

'I don't have a lover-boy.'

'Because you're too busy fawning over a paramedic.'

'I'm not fawning!'

'No?'

Reed sipped from a big red mug and raised an eyebrow at her, and in that moment she hated him with a passion. Why was he always there? Why was he always pushing her buttons? What did he get from that? Well, if it was a reaction he was chasing, she wasn't going to give him the satisfaction of getting one.

She sipped her own drink. Calmly. 'No.'

'Things are good between you and Tom?'

'Of course.'

'Hah! You paused!'

'I did not!' she protested.

Reed laughed, settling back in his seat. 'Oh, but you did! Something's going on. Come on, you can tell your Uncle Reed.'

'And have my personal life gossiped about throughout the station? Even more than it already is? No, thanks.'

'So there *is* something. You've just confirmed it. Hmm, what could it be?' He seemed to think for a bit. 'You finally told him you fancied him and he turned you down?'

So Reed thought it too? That she was too manly for any man to want her?

Only Tom seemed to fancy her no problem…
This was *her* issue. Not Tom's.

Feeling humiliated, she turned away from
Reed.

'Was I right?' Reed asked, looking shocked.
'Wow, I can't believe it. I really thought he
liked you, too. Would have put money on it.
I guess you can't always know a person, can
you? Want me to kick his arse for you?'

She turned to look at him, tears in her eyes,
grateful, suddenly, for his support. He might
rub her up the wrong way most days, and he'd
got this totally wrong, but he was there for
her. She was part of his team and they were
a family.

'Thanks, but, no. It's not like that and I
need to handle this on my own.'

'All right. But if you want me to stand
in the background—all menacing, like… I
could hold an axe and everything. Just say
the word.'

Cara didn't get time to laugh. The station
bell began to ring and they both leapt up to
respond, running from the kitchen, down
the stairs and into their firefighter uniforms.
They got into the fire engine just as Hodge
arrived with a slip of paper from the printer,
outlining the job.

'House fire.'

Cara nodded, strapping herself in, switching from personal mode to work mode. No matter what was happening between her and Tom, she had to forget it for now. Somewhere out there, someone might be about to lose everything.

And she knew how that felt.

Tom had been dispatched to a house fire on a busy council estate. The area, he knew, was compacted. Lots of high-rise council flats, all packed tightly together, with the exception of a few terraces of two-bedroomed houses, built in the Victorian era. If it was one of those, then there would be the possibility of multiple casualties, as a fire in one of them would spread easily to the homes either side.

He was glad to have some work to do. So far, it had been a quiet shift. Not that he liked to use the Q word. There was a superstition amongst health workers that you never said it out loud. Like actors didn't like to say *Macbeth*. It tempted fate and fate wasn't something you wanted to play around with.

As he came roaring into Gardenia Street he realised he was behind Cara's fire engine. He had no idea if she was on today, but he hoped so. It would be nice just to speak to her and reassure her that everything was fine, that nothing had to change yet if she didn't want it to.

They were getting close to their destination, and thankfully he couldn't see any plumes of smoke billowing into the air. Maybe it was a small fire? Maybe the residents had already contained it?

But when he pulled up at the address and they all got out of their vehicles they saw a bunch of teenagers at the end of the street on their bikes, laughing and catcalling and whooping it up.

Malicious call? He knew they couldn't just assume that. They still had to check.

He saw Hodge in his white helmet, going over to the house in question and knocking on the door. He hung back, waiting, aware that Cara stood off to one side, beside Reed, who was looking at him strangely. He tried to send a smile to say hello, but Reed just stared back.

Odd…

The door was opened by a woman in a dirty bathrobe, a cigarette held between her fingers. She looked surprised to see Hodge, almost taking a step back when she saw the array of emergency vehicles parked outside her home.

'Yeah?

'Madam, we've received a call that there is a fire in this property,' Hodge said.

'What? No!' She took a step outside, saw the kids at the end of the street. 'Those little bleeders! Wait till I get my hands around their scrawny necks!'

'Am I to understand that everything is fine?'

'Course it is!'

'Can we come in to check?'

'What for? I told ya! It's them kids! They've been winding me up all week. I've had it up to here…' She raised her hand above her head, before backing away and slamming the door shut.

Tom let out a sigh. It was a malicious call, by all accounts. Why did people do this? It was such a waste of resources, and whilst they were driving to a fake emergency it was taking the services away from someone who might desperately need a fire engine or an ambulance. Timewasters could kill someone, and when this sort of things happened it infuriated him.

He glanced over at Cara, caught her eye. He saw her look away briefly, then she took off her helmet and walked towards him. He saw Reed grab her arm and say something in a low voice to her, but she shook her head.

'I'll be fine,' she said.

What was that about? Had she told Reed what had happened? Why would she do that?

As Cara came towards him he felt his heart begin to race. He didn't want to mess this up. 'You all right?'

She nodded, not making eye contact. 'I'm fine.'

'Everything okay between you and Reed?' The firefighter was still glaring at him for some reason.

'He just wants to protect me.'

Understanding came. 'From me?'

'He could see that I was distracted this morning.'

Tom sighed. 'Look… I'm sorry about last night. I pushed. I pushed too fast and you weren't ready. I didn't mean to upset you and I don't want things to be awkward between us. You mean too much to me. Can we go back to the way things were before that?'

Now she looked at him. 'I'd like that.'

'I care a lot for you, Cara. I need you to know that.'

Her cheeks flushed and he liked how it made her look.

'Are we still on to meet at Mango tonight?' she asked uncertainly.

'Dance practice? Sure.'

That made him happy. He'd thought she might cancel. This way they could spend some more time together. It would give them time to talk about what had happened. Or what hadn't happened. If she wanted to. He was wary of pushing her. Wary of scaring her. That Leo must really have done a number on her.

'Okay. Well, good… I guess I'll see you later, then.' She smiled hesitantly and went to walk away.

He watched her clamber back into the fire engine. Watched the fire engine drive away. He called into Control. Reported it as a malicious call and notified them that he was ready and open for anything else.

He'd not been driving for more than two minutes, when a report of a suspected cardiac arrest came through, and he turned on the sirens and raced to his next call.

She almost cancelled. Nerves had got the better of her. Did she really want to see Tom again so soon? Did she really want to see Daphne? But this was their last session. They were meant to be learning turns and fleckerls and transitions, so that their changes of direction looked smooth.

She was beginning to doubt if she could go

through with this. Beginning to think she'd made a huge mistake in allowing something to happen between them. Because although she wanted to be with Tom more than anything, she was scared that at the last moment he wouldn't be physically attracted to her—even though he'd told her so many times that she was beautiful, and that what Leo had said had been more about him being a lousy, stupid idiot than it had been about her.

She wanted to believe that. She'd tried to believe that. But...the sting was still there. The doubt.

Cara craved love. Love for who she was. What she was. Love. Acceptance. Pure and simple.

Her father's love was so overbearing it was suffocating, so she ran from it. Her mother's love had been conditional, and so she'd run from it. Leo's love—though you could hardly even call it that—had been critical, and so she'd run from it.

Tom? Tom was meant to be different. He wasn't meant to be like the others. But would Tom always judge her against Victoria? The perfect, slender, soft, feminine Victoria.

Why was finding love so difficult? Why was it this hard?

Could she really afford to risk losing the

man she thought of as her best friend, and probably Gage, too? She wanted to punch something because she felt it was so unfair! If she were at the gym she'd tape up her knuckles and go at the punchbag for a few rounds, that was for sure!

She looked up at the windows of the Mango Dance Studio. She could hear music playing. Something hip-hop…the steady drive of a resounding bass note that practically made the windows reverberate.

I can back out of this. I can walk away. I don't have to go to the ball—I'll just make a donation to the Websters.

But something pushed her onwards and she opened the door, walked slowly up the stairs as if she was a guilty person on her way to the gallows, and entered the studio.

Naomi, the same receptionist was on, and she greeted her kindly and told her to go straight through. That Tom and Daphne were already there.

Oh, God! Tom and Daphne know each other well. Has Tom told Daphne what happened?

Because Daphne would surely hate her, then.

Her steps faltered, but then a small voice

in her head said, *No. You've done nothing wrong. Yet.*

So she pushed open the studio door and walked in, smiling, and sent a wave over to Tom, who stood with Daphne by the piano.

Tom's face broke into a smile and he trotted over to her. 'Hey, glad you made it. I was beginning to think you weren't coming.'

'I said I would,' she said, accepting the kiss that he planted on her cheek.

'Good, good… Okay, let's get started. I hope you two have been practising your steps?' Daphne asked, pointing a remote at the sound system, which began to play a classical waltz. 'Let's get you into hold. Show me what you remember.'

Cara hesitantly took Tom's hand and tried to get into position, looking away, over her left shoulder. She didn't want to think of elongating her neck *'as if a man is kissing it'*, as Daphne had said, because when she'd actually done that it had led to her fleeing Tom's home in shame.

'What's this gap?' Daphne protested, pushing Cara's body closer to Tom's. 'I could drive a lorry through there!'

It was hard holding Tom's hand, being pressed against him, when it was both all she'd ever wanted and also the one thing that she couldn't bear right now. With Daphne watching, the whole thing felt excruciating.

Daphne stood in Cara's eyeline and frowned. 'You had this so perfectly the other day! Have you forgotten everything?'

No. I've just got scared.

'Okay, let's see those box steps. And...*go!*'

Cara tried to remember her steps, tried to use the grace that she'd developed in the last lesson, but it was like starting anew. She felt so awkward and uncomfortable in Tom's arms that she immediately stepped on his toes and broke hold to step back and say sorry.

'Back in hold!' Daphne ordered.

She took his hand again, tried the steps, stepped on his toes again, flushed, felt heat rise all over her. Felt as if she might cry.

'What is going on? You had this the other day? What has changed?' Daphne frowned.

'It's okay. We've got this,' Tom tried to re-assure her. 'Cara? Look at me.'

She did so, feeling it was almost unbearable. To look at the man she loved and to know that he might yet reject her, and then she'd lose everything.

'Feel the music. Forget the steps. Let's just try going with the flow,' said Daphne.

She went back into hold and tried, making mistake after mistake, but gritted her teeth and pushed through. This was meant to be enjoyable! This was meant to be fun! Once upon a time the idea of dancing with Tom had been exciting! Being in his arms... Pressed up close... Only now it was like a nightmare and...

Her nose twitched. Could she smell *smoke*?

She broke hold and stepped back, sniffing the air.

'No, no, no! Back into hold,' ordered Daphne. 'You were getting there!'

'I can smell smoke,' she said.

'What?'

She wasn't imagining things. There was definitely a smell of something burning. She was attuned to it. Knew something wasn't right.

At that moment, the receptionist ran into the room. 'There's a fire next door!'

'Call the fire brigade,' Cara ordered, turning to usher Tom and Daphne from the room. 'Exit the building. Let's make sure everybody's out. Do you have a headcount?'

Daphne seemed to hesitate. 'There's a register for each class.'

'I'll need them. Get everyone out.'

Cara rushed from the studio, grabbing the clipboards with a class register on each. She ordered Tom to get Daphne out, whilst she went from studio to studio to make sure everyone else was out. It didn't take long. The three studios had already been alerted and everyone had left the building. Cara went outside and told them all to line up on the opposite side of the street, so they could take a headcount. No one was missing.

She turned to look at the fire. It had broken out in the empty building next door and looked to be on the first floor, flames already billowing at the windows...

Oh, my God...

It wasn't empty. There were people in those windows, banging on the glass. Were they trapped?

'Stay here!' she ordered everyone, then ran across the road and used a chair from outside a café to break the glass of the building's door.

'Cara!' Tom shouted. 'Wait for the fire brigade!'

But she couldn't wait. Those people didn't have time and there still might be a way to get them out.

She knew fire. She knew how to read it. She understood about flashpoints and backdraughts and all the dangers inherent in running into a burning building.

Only this time she wasn't wearing her

flame-retardant kit. This time she didn't have breathing apparatus strapped to her back, an oxygen mask upon her face. She could feel the smoke already getting into her lungs and throat and she coughed, looking for a stair-case. There was one right at the back of the building. Cement, so it wouldn't burn or collapse. She ran up the stairs, pulling her shirt over her mouth to help filter the air. At the top was a door and it was locked.

Damn!

She looked about her, saw a fire extin-guisher on the wall. It was probably out of date, but it would do. She hefted it in her hands and used it to bash open the lock, kick-ing the door open with her foot.

Flames billowed from each side of her. There were rags and bags on the floor. And what looked like a camping gas tank. Squat-ters? Had they been using it? It hadn't blown up, but there was a danger of that. She used the fire extinguisher to try and put out some of the flames and fought past them to get to the people at the window.

'Hey! This way!'

'Oh, my God! I thought we were going to die!'

Some of the people rushed past her, leav-ing behind a woman who was coughing so badly she could barely stand. Cara rushed over to her and hefted her easily over one shoulder, then began heading back the way she had come.

As she made her way down the stone steps she heard a fire crew arriving and saw the familiar sight of an appliance screeching to a halt outside. Tom was there too.

'I'm a paramedic,' he explained to the unknown fire crew.

Cara was coughing madly—could feel the smoke and the soot lining her throat, her eyes burning and watering madly.

'Cara? Are you okay?' Tom asked.

'I'm fine,' she managed to get out, coughing more and more, knowing her lungs needed to try and expel the deadly carcinogens that she'd breathed in during the rescue.

'You need to be checked out.'

'I'm fine. Just look after her.' She indicated the woman.

It was odd to stand back and watch the fire crew work. Despite her almost deadly inability to breathe properly, she yearned to be part of them—running in, dousing the flames, bringing the fire under control. There was something awesome about doing that. Controlling something that was so wild and untameable. Having to stand out here and do nothing made her feel useless.

But I wasn't. I still saved a life.

Paramedics arrived to take the woman away, and another draped a blanket around Cara and steered her towards their ambulance to get some oxygen. She sat there, feeling her breathing get steadily easier, until she no longer needed oxygen therapy.

The fire had been quickly contained and now it was time for the clean-up. She watched as everyone did their job.

Tom finally clambered into the ambulance with her and sat down beside her. He laid his hand on hers and squeezed it before letting go.

'You scared the hell out of me when you ran into that building.'

'I knew what I was doing.'

'Did you? You weren't in your kit. You could have been hurt, or killed.'

'But I wasn't. I'm fine.'

'If you'd have ended up in hospital…hurt… on a ventilator… If I'd had to see you like that…'

She looked at him then. Frowned. 'You didn't. You won't.'

'When I saw you carrying that woman

out…' His voice trailed off and he looked into the distance and grimaced.

Oh. It must have been a stark reminder to him that she was just as Leo said. Too masculine for any man to want her. He'd seen her in her firefighter's outfit often, had seen her fight fires—but had he ever been witness to her physical strength? The woman she'd carried out hadn't been little. It had taken all her strength to lift her over her shoulder.

But perhaps it was easier this way? Because now he wouldn't see her naked, and she wouldn't have to be vulnerable and have her heart torn in two by him.

'It's okay. I understand,' she said, trying to make it easy on him. Trying to give him a way out.

Because she wanted to make this easy on him. Then it would be easier on her. They could still be friends. Forget that kiss. Forget the fact that she felt love for him. Admit that all they ever would be was friends. That way she would still be able to see him. That way she could still see Gage. No reason why that darling little boy should miss out, just because the adults had screwed up.

'We both have such risky jobs, but yours is…' Tom shook his head. 'Dangerous! You run into burning buildings, you risk your life, and I… I need stability. Not just for me, but for Gage. He's already lost his mother. I… I'm meant to protect him. Put my son first. And what have I been doing? Chasing after you…'

'Chasing after you…'

As if she was a terrible choice he had made. She nodded, with tears dripping down her cheeks. She could hear in his voice what he was trying to say. He was ending this. Whatever it was that they had begun. And he was right. Gage had to come first.

'That's fine. I understand. It's probably best. You're right.'

She tried to put on a brave smile, though inside her heart was breaking.

CHAPTER NINE

APART FROM AN irritating cough, Cara was suffering no ill effects from going into the fire without her equipment. The cough she could deal with. That was fine. If she had to cough for the rest of her life she'd do it. But the feeling she had in her heart at realising that she and Tom could never be was something much more devastating.

She should have realised from the start! Tom could never love her. He was right. He had to put his son first. And she…? She was not good enough for him.

She'd hoped for so much more, but everyone in her life had been right. People had tried to tell her ever since she was a small girl that she didn't act the way a woman should.

Her mother had tried. For years!

'Wear a dress, Cara! Please. For me.'

'No one will notice you if you dress like a boy all the time.'

'Let's do something pretty with your hair.'

Cara had wriggled free of every attempt to make her more feminine.

Then there'd been Leo. He'd liked the novelty of going out with a female firefighter at first. He'd had a few bragging rights. He'd seemed to enjoy that. But when their relationship had become physical he'd not seemed to want her that much.

She'd not understood it. They'd been young. In their twenties. They ought to have been in the prime of their lives. But Leo had begun distancing himself from her after that first time, and she'd wondered if she'd done something wrong. He'd been her first. She'd adored him. She hadn't wanted anything to go wrong between them. And then he'd told her the truth.

'I'm not physically attracted to you.'

'You're too hard.'

'You've got more muscle than me.'

And now Tom. He didn't want her for who she was. Maybe if she'd chosen any other career than firefighter they might be together now.

She was too strong. Too masculine. Too dangerous.

If was off-putting to some—she got that. Had heard it her entire life.

She'd not thought Tom would be like that.

She stared out of the window of the fire engine as it raced to a fire in a block of flats. Normally, with the sirens going, she could block out what was happening in her personal life. She could enter work mode. But today she was considering her choices in life.

Would it have been different if she'd been more girly? If she'd gone into charity work? Worn skirts and dresses? Not gone to the gym and pumped iron? Not got any tattoos? Maybe if she'd paid more attention to being like other women she'd have true love by now? Maybe if she'd become a 'lady who lunched' she'd be with Tom now, because then she wouldn't pose a threat.

Who am I kidding? If I was a lady who lunched Tom and I would never have met.

Ahead of them, thick smoke billowed into the sky. This was a real fire. Not a malicious call. Residents of the block of flats were gathered in front of the burning building, hands over their mouths in disbelief, some crying, some coughing.

Their appliance pulled up and immediately Cara jumped out to provide assistance. She was tasked with finding out how many people—if any—might still be inside the burning flats.

One of the tenants, a middle-aged guy in his forties, ran his hand through his hair. 'I don't know… Er… I don't see Jason from flat ten—that's on the third floor. And the Kimbles? I don't see them. There's Tansy…she's a single mum…got a small boy…only four. They live next door to Jason.'

'What's his name?'

'Khaya.'

'Okay.'

She thought she heard someone call her name, but she forged inside, breathing apparatus on, and began to search the premises methodically.

It could feel claustrophobic, searching for people in a burning building. Vision was often limited by thick, choking smoke, and being clad in heavy kit and breathing apparatus was hard work. And you often didn't fit in small spaces. Ceilings could come crashing down around you, floors could give way, so you had to go at a careful pace, always checking your exit route, inching forward to rescue those who still might be trapped.

'You run into burning buildings…'

Behind her was Reed, and he headed left down a corridor as she headed right. Some people had left their doors open when they'd fled, so she was able to get inside easily, scan

the property and then move on to the next.
Others had locked their doors, but she managed to open them with a couple of swift
kicks, slamming the doors into the walls behind.

She was on the second floor. The missing
people were from the third. But she couldn't
miss checking this floor in case someone had
been missed. She would never forgive herself if someone died because she hadn't done
her job.

Tom had called Cara's name as she'd run
into the burning building, his heart sink-
ing into his stomach. This was a fierce fire.
The building looked as if it could collapse at
any moment. A fragile prefabricated building, built in the seventies, it probably hadn't
been brought up to code in an age, what with
council cutbacks...

He'd arrived right behind Green Watch.
Had run over to the residents to see if anyone
needed medical help. He'd seen Cara talking to someone and had tried to catch her
eye, needing to talk to her. Things had been
left pretty awkwardly yesterday, after his
outburst, and then he'd had to take Daphne
home.

And now she was gone again.

What if something happened to her in that building?

He'd been stupid yesterday. Not thinking about Cara's feelings, only absorbed in his own confusing ones. The guilt he'd been feeling about wanting another woman. The fear he had about ruining his friendship with Cara. The fear of losing her—of having to sit by her bedside if she got injured during a shout.

And then last night he'd been chatting with Gage before bedtime?

'I wish Cara were here all the time, Daddy,' he'd said.

'You do?'

Gage had nodded. Yawned. *'I like playing with her. Do you, Daddy?'*

'Yeah. I do.'

'Good. 'Cos sometimes you're sad and I think Cara makes us better.'

And that had made him think about how much Cara loved his son.

Seeing her carry that unconscious woman out of the building had reminded him of how strong she was. Not just physically, but mentally. Her determination to put others before herself was one of her greatest traits.

If only it was that simple. She runs into burning buildings.

They could collapse. This block of flats could collapse, with her inside, and he would lose everything all over again!

He couldn't do that.

And he certainly wouldn't put Gage through it.

But his heart thudded against his ribcage as he waited for Cara to emerge from the building all the same. His head might be wary of the risks in getting too close to Cara Maddox, but his heart had only ever known how to love her.

Cara paired up with Reed as they took the stairway to the third floor. The stairs were concrete, the only part of the building not on fire, yet still the air billowed with smoke that curled and danced to its own tune.

As they reached the fire door to the third floor they could see flames roaring when they looked through the small window.

'We stay together!' Reed shouted.

She nodded, yanking the door open and hugging the wall that would take them through the flames down to the two flats on the left-hand side.

The heat was fierce. Sweat was pouring down her back, but she barely noticed. They made it to the first door, saw smoke issuing out from behind it, indicating a possible active fire beyond. The door was locked. Reed gave it a hefty kick and they were in.

There was a long corridor, with rooms going off it left and right, thick with black smoke and flashes of orange and red. Cara heard something shatter, off to her left, and entered the first room. Empty. She checked beneath the bed, inside the wardrobes—anywhere someone might think was a good place to hide.

Nothing.

They moved on. Found a bathroom with the door locked. Another kick and it came open easily, and inside was a man, cowering in the bathtub fully clothed, water running over him.

'You Jason?' Cara yelled through her mask.

He nodded.

'Come with me,' Reed said, grabbing his arm and pulling him out. Before he left, he turned back to Cara. 'Be safe!'

'I will!'

With one missing person found, Cara knew they were not going to find the Kimble family in this flat. They were next door, the tenant had said, but she still had to sweep this flat. She entered the room at the end of the hall. A living room, with a small kitchenette off to one side. The ceiling had fallen through here and fire raged above. There were collapsed struts and beams lying haphazardly on the floor, smoking wildly. But there were no other people here.

Cara backed out of the flat and went on to the last one on this floor. The door was closed, but it felt hot. There had to be a fire raging behind it.

She kicked it open and stood back, waiting for the surge of flame, watching as it licked up to the roof beyond. Could she hear something? Screams? Someone crying for help?

She kept low and made her way in, her arm above her head to protect it from any falling debris. It was hard to see in here. The smoke was thick. She got out her torch and switched it on. A television still played in the living room—she could see the flicker of images—and by the window stood a woman, holding a small child in her arms. A child who looked unconscious.

Cara carefully made her way forward, jumping to one side as the ceiling above her collapsed, raining burning plaster and wood down on her. She fell, slamming into the wall, but soon was kicking off the burning joist and getting back to her feet, finally making it to the Kimbles.

'Tansy? Khaya?'

The woman turned, her face filled with fear. 'I can't wake him!'

'It's the smoke.'

Cara took the boy and laid him down, where the smoke was thinnest. She pulled off a flame-retardant glove and touched her fingers to the boy's neck. There was a pulse, thankfully.

Behind them, the ceiling crashed down completely, blocking their exit with a roaring flame. There was no way they could go back the way Cara had come in. They would have to find another way.

The window was slightly ajar, but didn't fully open. Cara looked around, saw a wooden chair, and told Tansy to stand back. She picked up the chair and swung it at the glass, shattering it into a million pieces, then she cleared away the last remaining shards around the frame and peered out to see if the ladders were being sent up.

They were!

Cara flashed her torch and waved to her crew below, indicating that she had two people to rescue.

Hodge was coming up the ladder, with Garrett behind. One for each of them.

Cara dipped back inside and took off her

breathing mask. She secured it to Khaya's face, then double-checked the window frame once again, to make sure that no one would suffer a nasty cut as they were carried out through the window.

'Nearly out,' she reassured Tansy.

'I'm afraid of heights!' she yelled back, coughing.

'You'll be okay. Don't worry.'

Cara covered Tansy's body with her own as the flames continued to get near. Then Hodge was at the window and Cara passed out Khaya. Garrett was there too, and they gently coached the petrified Tansy out onto the ladder. As something exploded behind her Cara ducked, feeling something explode as it flew past her.

What the hell was that?

But then she was up at the window and climbing onto the rescue ladder herself.

It slowly began to lower. And the air became cleaner and easier to breathe. Cara let out a heavy sigh. They'd done it. They'd got everyone out, as far as they knew. If there was anyone else still missing it would be up to the others to find them. She knew Hodge wouldn't let her go in again—not until she'd been checked medically.

She saw Tom at the bottom of the ladder,

waiting for his patients to be brought down. His face was etched in a deep frown. She wished she could run into his arms and just hold him, tell him she was safe and hear him say, *Thank God. I was so worried about you!*

But she knew that was never going to happen. If she wanted someone like Tom then she would have to change who she was, and she wasn't sure she could do that. It would all be pretend. She'd be playing dress-up—something she'd hated ever since she was a child.

No. She would have to look elsewhere for love.

Or maybe she was destined to be alone for ever.

As they reached the ground, Tom set to working on Khaya immediately.

'Is he going to be okay?' she asked, knowing how hard this must be for him. Working on a child the same age as Gage.

Tom looked up at her, his face strained. 'I'm doing my best.'

He was right. He had a job to do. Save the boy, not answer her inane questions! Angry with herself, she walked away, back to the appliance, where her feelings about everything that had happened lately threatened to overwhelm her.

Tears in her eyes, she lashed out, kicking the tyre of the fire engine over and over again.

It was the day of the charity ball for the Websters. Her mother's birthday. Cara's night. She was supposed to be going with Tom on her arm, looking like a lady.

What a joke that was going to be!

They'd both know that she wasn't, and everyone else would too. All her family would be there, no doubt laughing about her behind her back. And all her fire crew family. Reed would no doubt have something to say. And Tom? He would probably feel the most awkward of all.

If he showed up.

She'd not heard from him since he'd called things off between them. This was the longest they'd ever gone without speaking. She'd tried texting, but had got no response. She'd even left a message on his voicemail. Surely he wasn't going to stand her up for this? However wrong things had gone between them romantically, he was still supposed to be her best friend.

She'd hoped for so much more from Tom. That he would *see* her. That he would see the woman she was beneath the firefighter's suit.

Yes. She was totally different from Victoria. They could never be compared. Clearly. But they'd had something…hadn't they? Apparently not.

Maybe she was just terrible at reading men. She'd made a bad choice yet again.

Will I ever learn?

Still, Tom deserved to be with someone who didn't put her life at risk every day. She couldn't expect him to live like that. Wondering if she'd make it home every day. She'd witnessed the trauma he'd gone through after his wife's death, so she understood his reticence as his heart began to get involved.

Cara sighed. It was time to put on the dress. Do her hair. Make-up. Wear those dreaded heels! Instead, she checked her phone again. Surely Tom should have called her by now? Or maybe his silence was telling her all that she needed to know? That he wasn't going to show. That she would have to walk into her childhood home without a date on her arm?

She sat down in front of her mirror and started combing her hair, trying to decide which was the best way to wear it.

If she could get out of this night right now she would. But she'd made a promise and she wouldn't go back on it. And if she turned up alone and anyone had anything to say about it, then she'd just lift her chin, square her shoulders, and walk away.

She decided to wear her hair up. She'd been to the shops and bought some fancy pins. But every time she tried to make her hair stay put, it kept falling down.

How do other girls do this?

In the end she resorted to an instructional video she found online.

Ah. That's how.

She'd been doing it all wrong…she needed to put it up in sections, not all at once.

It looks pretty.

Next, she got out the make-up palette that she'd bought at the same time as the pins, wincing at the extortionate cost, and sought another online tutorial for something called 'a smoky eye'.

The first attempt made her look like a panda, and then she'd begun to cry, so she had to wipe it all off with wet wipes. But the second time was much better.

I'm a quick learner.

She put in some stud earrings she already had, and then slipped out of her robe and put on the dress. It clung to her in all the right places and she sat down to put on the heels. When she looked in the mirror to check out her reflection, she gasped. She'd never seen the entire look put together at the same time! It was astonishing! It was…*dizzying!* Suddenly she understood why girls did this. They could change who they were. Show different sides of themselves. Looking as if she ought to be walking down a red carpet made her feel…*special.*

Suddenly she wished her mother was there to see it. She would have been proud. She would have cried, without a doubt, and Cara knew that because she felt like crying again, too.

'What do you think, Mum?' she said to the empty room.

Of course there was no answer.

What would Tom do, seeing her look like this? Would he have second thoughts?

No. It takes more than a pretty dress and some heels to change a man's mind.

She checked the time. The car would be here at any moment to collect her. Tom ought to be here, only he wasn't, and the rejection she felt was absolute.

She sniffed, realising that she had to put this disaster with Tom behind her. It hadn't worked. They'd both been stupid to think that they could take their friendship and make it into something more. She could only be a stereotypical woman for this one night, and Tom would want someone who could be beautiful and feminine for ever.

There was a knock at her door.

Cara answered it. Her father's chauffeur, Jamison, was waiting.

'Lady Cara.' He gave a brief nod of his head. 'You look stunning.'

'Thank you, Jamison.'

She closed the door and walked down the path, feeling terribly alone, unaware of the ringing phone in her hallway.

The car carried her up the long driveway and she let out a small sigh at seeing her childhood home once again. She had lots of great happy memories of here. Playing in the stables. Going horse riding. Making dens with her brothers and playing hide and seek in all the attic spaces. Cara could hear her mum's voice now, calling to them all to come down for tea. She missed it. Missed her. Wished she'd had the opportunity to show her how she looked today.

I may have totally ballsed up my love-life, Ma, but look at me in a dress!

She had no doubt her mother would have squealed in delight at seeing her. She would have wanted to take many pictures. Pictures that would have been framed and set in pride of place for everyone to see.

Lady Cara Maddox. How she was supposed to be.

But she'd never fitted into anyone else's mould. Cara had always done her own thing and walked tall, and she would walk tall now, no matter what anyone said. Even if it meant walking in her own lane…even if it meant that she walked alone.

Suddenly the car door was being opened and her father was there. 'Cara! Look at you! Oh, my gosh, you're so beautiful.'

Her father took her by both hands and kissed both cheeks, before stepping back to take another look.

'Stunning. Simply stunning.' He smiled at her, proud, then looked behind her and frowned. 'No gentleman paramedic?'

She shook her head, determined not to cry. 'He couldn't make it.'

She had no idea if it was the right thing to say. Maybe it would have been better to say he was running late? But then when he didn't show at all, she'd get those knowing, pitying looks.

Poor Cara. Lost another guy, huh?

This way, if he did show up—which she

doubted very much now—it would actually be a pleasant surprise.

'That's a pity. Everything all right between you two?' her father pressed.

'It's fine.'

'All right. But I can't have my daughter having no one to dance with tonight. You'll dance with me, and then I think Xander or maybe Tarquin will want to whisk you around the dance floor looking like that.'

'I'm quite happy not being on the dance floor, Dad. These heels aren't best suited to fancy footwork.'

'Nonsense! Your mother danced in heels, and you've been practising, by all accounts!'

He disappeared into the crowd before she could find out who had told him she'd been practising the waltz.

Cara gazed out over the ballroom. It looked magnificent, as always. Tall marble columns stood all around the edge of the room. Long, red velvet curtains hung in between. Beautiful paintings and portraits of Maddox ancestors adorned the walls. The dance floor was filled with couples—men in tuxedos, women in all colours. It was like watching a garden of flowers, dancing in the breeze. To one side was an orchestra, currently playing a gentle number, and in between them all uniformed butlers and waitresses mingled, offering flutes of champagne and trays of hors-d'oeuvres.

She was surrounded by people, but she'd never felt so lonely.

'Can we get there any faster?' asked Tom from the back seat of the cab, trying his best to tie his bow tie, but failing terribly.

'Traffic, my friend. Nothing I can do,' said the cab driver, chewing his gum.

They were in a long stream of cars waiting to go up the long drive to Higham Manor and, unable to wait a moment longer, he flung some notes at the cabbie, darted from the car and began to run—with a large box under his arm.

He'd been a fool. An absolute fool! Thinking that if he removed Cara from his life he wouldn't have to worry about her. Since telling her he couldn't be with her, he'd not been able to get her out of his mind. And then there'd been that conversation with Gage…

'We…er…won't be seeing much of Cara from now on,' he'd told him.

Gage had looked shocked. Then sad. *'Why?'*
'Because…'

He'd struggled to think of a way to explain it to his son that he would understand. But that had been hard when he still wasn't sure he understood his own feelings.

'Because she's busy.'

'Has she got a new job?'

'No.'

'Then why can't she see us? She's always seen us. Always played with me and read me bedtime stories.'

'I know. It's just that things happen when you're a grown-up and life gets complicated.'

'If she came to live here then it wouldn't matter if she was busy.'

He'd stared at his son. *'What?'*

Gage had stared up at his father with wide eyes. *'I want to be able to see Cara!'*

'She has a dangerous job, son. She might...' His words had got caught in his throat.

'Might die? Like Mummy did?'

He'd nodded, barely able to speak at such a thought.

Gage had been quiet for a while, then he'd sat up in bed and said, *'Daddy? If she can be brave, then we can too.'*

He'd stared at his son, surprised at the wisdom that came from a four-year-old boy. He'd been avoiding Cara's calls, sitting on the stairs as his phone rang with her name on the caller ID. He'd hated himself for ignoring them, knowing he needed to keep his commitment to their fake date at the ball but not knowing how he was going to bear the pretence now that things were over between them.

But now Gage had made him think that maybe it could be different.

Cara was a firefighter. She'd always wanted to be a firefighter. That was who she was and he loved her for it. And, yes, she was brave. Perhaps braver than them all. She'd defied everyone who had tried to change her and stuck to her guns. She had been there for him and his son in so many ways and he knew she had strong feelings for him. She had been devastated when he'd said they had to end.

Staying away from Cara for the rest of his life? That wasn't saving his heart—that was killing it! Why stay away when he could be with her? Any time he got to spend with her would be a gift. And if she got injured or, God forbid, something awful happened to her…? That would be terrible, obviously, and he didn't want to think of it happening at all. But if it did then he and Gage would have been blessed by having known her at all. Being part of the love that she gave so willingly.

So, yes. He'd been a fool and he needed to tell her.

She must be thinking he had backed out of their fake date. Well, he wasn't that kind of guy. He'd said he would be there and he was looking forward to dancing with her. Besides, they needed to talk about things.

When he reached the doors to the manor, he stopped, and asked a uniformed butler who was wearing a perfect bow tie if he could help him with his.

'Absolutely, sir.' The butler smiled patiently as he tied the tie, and then he reached into an inside jacket pocket. 'Might I suggest, sir…a comb?'

Tom glanced down at the man's hand and laughed. 'Yeah, thanks.' That was probably a good idea. 'Where's the ballroom?'

'Straight ahead, sir. Just follow the music.'

He nodded and walked towards the ballroom. When he got there someone presented him with a flute of champagne and he took it, downing it in one, before placing his empty glass back onto the tray.

He was looking for the most beautiful woman in the world, who would be wearing a gold dress.

His gaze scanned the walls, where groups of people stood in groups, chatting, but he couldn't see her there. Then he looked on the dance floor, and his eyes caught a glimpse of glittering gold and flaming red hair. She was dancing with her father.

Feeling his heart pound out of his chest, he stepped forward into the dancing throng. 'Excuse me... Sorry, could I just...? Excuse me...thank you.'

And then he was there, right next to her, and she looked stunning, if a little uncomfortable.

'Might I interrupt?'

Cara's head swivelled in his direction at the sound of his voice and she might even have gasped a little.

Her father smiled a greeting and nodded, stepping back. 'Of course. Be my guest.'

He stood in front of her, smiling. 'I'm sorry I missed your calls.'

'Where have you been?'

'Practising being an idiot. You look beautiful.'

She blushed.

'I've brought you a gift. I almost brought you a corsage, but then I saw this, so...' He proffered the large box that was tucked under his arm.

It was wrapped in gold, with a gold ribbon, which she tore open, smiling when she saw inside, nestled in white tissue paper, a sparkly pair of golden trainers.

'I thought these would let me dance with you for longer.'

She bent down to take off her hated heels and slip her feet into the trainers.

Tom took the heels, put them in the now empty box and passed it to a bewildered waitress. 'Could you get rid of these, please?'

The waitress took them and Cara stood up, gazing at him with apprehension. 'I thought you weren't coming.'

'I would never have missed this. I'm sorry I had you worried.'

He stared at her and stepped closer, holding out his hands for her to step into the hold they knew.

She did so.

And as she slipped hand into his he felt that somehow this was all going to be all right.

'I need to tell you how I feel about you,' he said.

She looked apprehensive. 'It's okay. I know. I'm not like Victoria. I never will be. But I am a firefighter and that will never change.'

'I'm not looking for another Victoria and I don't ever want you to change.' Tom waited for her to look at him. 'I've been an utter fool,' he said. 'A coward.'

'And I've been too caught up in myself,' she told him. 'I forgot you needed to think about Gage, too. My job makes me a risky prospect. I get caught up in what I do. I run towards danger. I go into burning buildings and I give up my oxygen and I use my body to protect others. Gage doesn't need someone like that. Neither do you.

'Are you kidding me? That selflessness? That bravery? Both of those things are wonderful! I would never change you. Not in a million years! You're perfect exactly as you are. And when I saw you carrying that woman from the burning building I realised just how much you terrified me.'

She frowned. Puzzled. 'What are you saying?'

'I'm saying that I realised I could have lost you, and that thought was too terrible to contemplate…because I'm in love with you.'

A small smile broke across her face. 'You're in love with me?'

'I am and I always will be. And I'd like to think that you will forgive me for running and being afraid, because I'm not any more, and I'd like to make this a real date between us. Not a fake one. What do you think to that?'

'I don't know what to say…'

She flushed, her cheeks pinker than he'd ever seen them before, and he just wanted to kiss her in front of everyone. Make it real.

Let everyone in this room know that he loved this woman. Because she was all woman. No matter if anyone else had made her feel that she was somehow lacking. She was the best woman. The only woman for him.

'Say you'll be my girlfriend for real?' He smiled, pulling her back into hold and pressing himself up against her, imagining more.

Cara laughed, and looked around her before looking back at him. 'I've loved you since the moment I met you, Tom. Do you know how hard that's been for me?'

He nodded. 'You still haven't answered my question.'

'What was that?'

'Will you be my girlfriend?'

She nodded, beaming. 'I will.'

'Good. Now kiss me. Kiss me before I spontaneously combust.'

Cara laughed, bringing her lips to his, and kissed him as he'd never been kissed before.

EPILOGUE

THE DOUBLE DOORS to her old childhood bedroom opened, and she turned just as her father gasped in surprise.

'Cara…you look beautiful,' he said in awe.

She flushed and turned to check her reflection in the long mirror. She was bedecked in white. A beautiful fishtail wedding gown with a sweetheart neckline, covered in lace and crystals. A diamond tiara and a long, floaty veil.

'Thanks.'

'If your mother were here…' His voice choked in his throat.

Cara reached out a hand to take his, squeezing his fingers in solidarity. She knew what he wanted to say.

If your mother were here, she'd be crying with happiness.

And he was right. She would be. Seeing her daughter like this. About to be married.

Looking like the perfect bride. The fact that her mother would not be with her at her wedding hurt a lot. But Cara knew that wherever she was she would be looking down at her and smiling, full of pride and joy.

'I wish she was here.'

Her father nodded. 'Me, too. You know, I'm very much aware that I've been a bit... *overpowering* at times. What do you call it? Sticking my nose in where it's not wanted?' He smiled.

Cara smiled back. 'A bit. But it doesn't matter today, Dad. Today is for happy memories.'

'You're right. But I wanted to have this moment before I pass your hand over to Tom to try and explain.'

He paused for a moment. Checked his own reflection in the mirror and rearranged his cravat. Plumping it to perfection.

'When your mother died, I was distraught. We all were, I know. But in you I saw your mother. You're so alike in so many ways. The way you smile. The way you tilt your head when you're listening to someone talk the way you're doing now.' He smiled again. 'The way you laugh. And when you moved out I couldn't bear to be separated from you. I still needed that contact with her through you.

I kept trying to mould you to be like her and I should have known better. You're your own woman, just as you should be, and I wanted to tell you today that I've realised what I was doing and it was wrong. So... I apologise.'

'Oh, Dad!' She stepped forward to wrap her arms around him and held him tight.

They stood in an embrace for a while, until the wedding planner, Harriet, came in with her clipboard, clapping her hands.

'Time's tight, people. Ready to go?'

Cara let go of her father and stepped back, just as he reached into his jacket pocket.

'Your something borrowed.' He passed her a velvet box.

She frowned in question, then opened it. Inside, lying on a green velvet cushion, was her mother's diamond necklace. 'Dad...'

'She'd want you to wear it. She wore it on her wedding day. But you know you don't have to, if you think I'm being—'

'Dad, it's perfect. I'd be honoured.' She turned so he could fasten it at the back of her neck.

Cara looked at it in the mirror. Her mother would always be with her, but this was extra-special and made her feel close to her once again.

'Ready to go?'

Her father held out his arm and she slid hers into it.

'I'm ready.'

Harriet left the room and signalled to someone at the bottom of the stairs. Music suddenly bloomed through the high hall and up the stairway of Higham Manor. The 'Wedding March'.

Cara took a brief moment to adjust her veil, so it lay perfectly, and then began the slow walk from her bedroom, all the way down the sweeping, staircase which was adorned with fresh flower garlands.

Beneath them in the grand hall were all their guests. Friends. Family. Work family. Everyone she knew. People whose lives she'd saved and stayed in touch with. Everyone. She saw all their happy faces, all their smiles, and saw how beautiful everyone looked. But there was one person she wanted to see the most.

Tom.

He stood in front of a flowered arch, dressed in a suit like her father's, his lovely face looking up to her as she descended the stairs. Beside him, in a miniature top hat and tails, stood Gage, holding a red cushion with their wedding rings on it.

Her heart pounded with joy as all her dreams began to come true.

People whispered their good wishes and love as she passed them. She met happy gaze after happy gaze. She got a cheeky wink from Reed. A bow of the head from Hodge.

And then she was standing next to Tom and her father was letting go of her and stepping back.

Tom reached for her hand, smiling. 'You look stunning.'

'Thanks,' she answered shyly.

'Are you wearing them?' he whispered.

Cara lifted up her skirt slightly, to reveal the bridal trainers that he'd bought for her. White. Studded with crystals that caught the light.

Tom laughed. 'You look perfect.'

She smiled, covering them up again. 'So do you.'

* * * * *

*If you enjoyed this story, check out
these other great reads from
Louisa Heaton*

Their Marriage Worth Fighting For
Their Marriage Meant to Be
A GP Worth Staying For
Twins for the Neurosurgeon

All available now!